# FATAL VENDETTA

## VANISHING RANCH
### BOOK 7

## CHRISTY BARRITT

ADDISON BARLOW TURNED off the lights in her cabin as she stood beside the window. Slowly, she peered around the edge, moving the curtain only by an inch.

She stared at the cabin next door.

The place was probably three hundred feet away. Close enough that she could see it, but far enough away that it was hard to make out any details.

She wasn't trying to be nosy.

But something was going on at her neighbor's place.

Earlier, Addie had met the woman staying there. Brianna was probably in her mid-twenties, and she'd seemed pleasant enough. But something haunted lurked behind the woman's eyes.

Addie recognized the look because she'd lived in that same troubled place before.

Who was she kidding?

She was living there now.

But she couldn't figure out exactly what was wrong. As the two of them had chatted about recipes, Brianna hadn't taken the opportunity to ask for help. But Addie had seen the bruises on her arms.

Just as Addie had gotten back to her cabin, a man in a truck pulled up. He had to be Bruce, Brianna's husband.

Addie had watched as the man climbed from his truck and stormed toward the cabin.

Once inside, the two of them had begun screaming at each other.

Addie couldn't make out the words. But their argument was heated, to say the least.

She'd started to call the police, but she'd stopped herself.

What would she say? Was this a domestic disturbance? Sure, it sounded like the two were having a major disagreement.

But that didn't mean anything criminal was happening. Couples screamed at each other all the time when they fought.

Addie didn't. She'd never again be with a man who yelled at her either.

Eventually, the screams at her neighbor's place had died.

An hour passed, and the argument started again.

Gathering her courage, Addie stepped away from the window and pulled on a coat.

She couldn't stand here and do nothing. She needed to know if she should call the cops or if she was overreacting.

The only way to find out was to get closer. To hear more details.

Remaining in the shadows, Addie crept toward the cabin.

The yelling became louder as she got closer, even though she still couldn't make out any words.

She circled around to the back deck and carefully climbed the old, wooden steps.

A creak sounded beneath her feet.

She paused as fear gripped her.

What would Hayes do if he were here?

Her estranged husband always seemed to know what to do. Decisions came naturally to him. Maybe it was what had made him such a good Homeland Security agent.

That confidence was one reason Addie had been drawn to him. The self-assurance she lacked, he made up for.

They'd balanced each other out.

She bit back a cry as the reality of her loss hit her again.

Hayes was no longer in her life, and she missed him terribly.

Addie needed to get used to doing life without him. Their split had been her choice, and now she needed to live with her decision.

But there was so much more than met the eye to the events that had unfurled . . .

She took another step, and then another until she reached the deck. Remaining low, she crept toward one of the windows where bright, cheery light escaped.

The whole place was an enigma as snow covered the steepled roof and smoke puffed from the chimney. The cabin looked like a cozy storybook picture.

Or maybe the place was more like Hansel and Gretel.

The argument floated outside.

"You don't know what you're talking about!" Brianna shouted.

"And you never listen! Why can't you just listen to me for once? Is it that hard?"

Addie peered around the wall and through the window, trying to remain in the shadows.

Sure enough, the man—Bruce, Addie assumed—and Brianna were quarreling. Bruce leered in Brianna's face. His cheeks were red, and veins bulged at his temples.

The next instant, his thick fingers wrapped around Brianna's arms as he jerked her closer.

"Unless you want to die, you need to listen to me—and listen closely," he muttered.

Addie gasped and reeled back in time as memories of her first marriage pummeled her. Her lungs tightened until she could hardly breathe, and panic claimed her muscles.

Staggering back, her foot hit something.

A bucket.

The metal container clamored to the ground.

She jerked her gaze back to the window.

Bruce had turned toward the sound.

He released Brianna and stormed toward the back door.

Toward Addie.

More fear pulsed through her.

Quickly, she scrambled off the deck and darted away.

Not toward her cabin.

She didn't want to let the man know where she was staying.

Instead, she headed toward the woods surrounding the backside of the lakefront property and ducked behind a juniper. She pressed herself against the tree and waited, praying he wouldn't find her.

Her pulse quickened with fear as the seconds ticked by.

How had she left trouble in one place only to find it here? Was she cursed?

As she peered around the tree, she spotted Bruce. He stalked toward the woods.

Toward her.

Even in the darkness, Addie could see his anger. His motions were stiff and heavy. His eyes narrow. His jaw set.

He paused and glanced around, his hands fisted at his sides.

Maybe he thought the sound was just a raccoon. They had those around here. Even bears visited on occasion. That's what Addie had read in that travel brochure left in her cabin.

She held her breath as she lifted fervent prayers. *Please, Lord. Protect me in my stupidity. Protect Brianna. Help!*

She remembered the verse she'd clung to for so long: *And we know that in all things God works for the good of those who love him, who've been called according to his purpose. Romans 8:28.*

Maybe she didn't love God enough. Maybe that's why nothing in her life ever seemed to work out.

Bruce remained planted at the edge of the woods as he surveyed everything around him.

Addie's heart pounded in her ears.

Maybe she should take this opportunity to run.

But her gut told her to stay put.

She wasn't sure if it was fear or logic that kept her frozen where she was. But she remained still and waited.

Finally, Bruce grunted, turned, and stomped back toward the cabin.

Addie wanted to feel relief—to let the air leave her lungs in a whoosh. But she couldn't.

Especially since she feared Brianna might be in danger.

As soon as Bruce disappeared back inside the cabin, Addie straightened.

Gathering her courage, she sprinted through the woods toward the safety of her cabin.

She had to figure out what to do.

If an innocent woman was suffering at the hands of an abusive man, Addie couldn't simply sit back and do nothing.

She had to help.

But how?

———

Hayes Barlow gripped the steering wheel of his rented SUV as he drove along the dark, mountainous road.

He hadn't expected the call from Addie.

Hadn't expected to hear the fear in her voice.

And he *definitely* hadn't expected her to ask for his help. Not after the way things had ended between them. Not considering the way she avoided him and wanted nothing to do with him—not even to talk.

But if Addie needed him, there was no way Hayes would say no.

Even if the woman had broken his heart when she'd told him she no longer loved him and that their marriage of nearly two years was done. In fact, their anniversary was in four days. He'd hoped to surprise her with a trip. That was no longer on the table.

He'd given up his job with Homeland Security a few months ago and had started working at a place called Vanishing Ranch. But after Hayes had gotten the call from Addie, he'd informed his boss he needed to attend to some personal business. She'd told him to go.

Thankfully, Hayes had been working a job in Reno, so he wasn't far away from Lake Tahoe—only about an hour. He'd grabbed his things, jumped into the SUV, and taken off.

These roads could be treacherous at any time of

the year. But Hayes knew as he got deeper into the mountains, he'd probably hit some snow. It was late November, and the snow had started falling on and off a month ago.

Still, he had no time to waste.

*I think my neighbor . . . she's in trouble. Her husband is hurting her. What should I do?*

That's what Addie had told him. Then she'd explained what happened.

Hayes had told Addie to stay in her cabin with the doors locked and not to open them until he got there and asked her to.

He could tell her to call the police, but he was doubtful they'd do anything.

Still, he feared for Addie. She had a big heart. Because of her abusive first husband, Hayes knew that any type of violence shook her up. As it should. As it should *anyone*.

A man should never lay a hand on a woman.

But Hayes's relationship with Addie . . .

He frowned as he gripped the steering wheel harder.

Their relationship was strained, to say the least.

Four months ago, she'd told him she wanted a divorce. Her announcement had come after she'd endured a terrifying home invasion, but Hayes still didn't understand her decision. He'd tried to win her back, to no avail.

That's why Hayes was so surprised she'd called him today.

He wasn't complaining. He'd do whatever it took to win Addie over again.

The road became narrower as he drove deeper into the Sierra Nevada Mountains. He'd come to this area of northeastern California once on a family vacation, but probably twenty years had passed since then.

What was Addie doing out here?

He'd wanted to ask her when she called, but the question didn't seem appropriate considering the gravity of the situation. Besides, maybe it wasn't his business. He was trying to respect her boundaries and give her space, but it was so hard sometimes.

Hayes's GPS showed he was getting close. He took a few more turns until finally his headlights illuminated a small cabin in the distance and the sparkling—but dark—lake beyond.

This place was in the middle of nowhere. Why in the world had Addie chosen this location? It didn't seem like a site a woman would want to travel to alone. The place was so remote Hayes was surprised she'd even had any cell phone service.

He stared at the cabin a moment.

All the lights inside were off, and darkness stared from the windows.

But Addie's car—a white Honda Accord the two of them had purchased together last year—waited out front.

This was definitely the right place.

Quickly, Hayes shut off his engine and climbed out. His gun was holstered at his shoulder, and he'd use it if he needed to.

But he hoped it didn't come down to that.

Glancing at the woods around the cabins, he saw nothing unusual. Yet his nerves were on edge.

Was it because Addie had made it sound as if danger lurked nearby? Or because his instincts somehow sensed the jeopardy around him?

He walked to the front door and gripped the handle.

It was locked.

Good. Addie had done exactly what he'd told her to do.

But, before he talked to her, he wanted to check the outside of this place.

Creeping around the cabin, he paused as his flashlight hit a footprint on the ground.

A footprint that didn't belong to Addie.

It was too big. Too deep. Too rugged.

But the indentation was fresh.

Someone else—a man—had recently been outside this cabin.

Fire raced through Hayes's blood at the thought.

He started back to the front door, now desperate to check on Addie.

But as he stepped around the corner, a shadow lunged at him.

The next instant, everything around him went black.

# CHAPTER
# TWO

ADDIE HEARD A NOISE OUTSIDE.

Was that a thump? A moan?

Fear shimmied down her spine.

She'd seen Hayes pull up. But he'd told her not to open the door until he said so.

For that reason, she'd remained pressed against the wall, clutching a butcher knife in her hand.

Just in case.

Coming to this secluded area had seemed like a good idea at first. A friend from her exercise studio owned it and had offered to let Addie use it.

But seclusion could be a blessing or a curse.

Right now, the isolation felt like a curse.

Leaning toward the window, she peered outside in the direction of the sound.

She gasped when she saw a figure in black running toward the lake.

As her gaze traveled downward, she thought she saw someone on the ground.

Panic pulsed through her.

Hayes.

*Hayes* lay on the ground.

Suddenly, she forgot all his instructions.

Still gripping the knife, she darted toward the door. With trembling fingers, she unlocked it. Then she raced outside toward Hayes.

He moaned as he sat up. His broad shoulders were obscured by the thick coat he wore. Those brown eyes she loved so much were squinched with pain. His dark hair looked tousled.

But mostly she noticed how he clutched his head.

Someone must have hit him.

"Are you okay?" She set her knife down on the rocky ground and knelt beside him.

"You shouldn't have come out here." Hayes's eyes narrowed—either with pain or irritation. Possibly both. "It's not safe."

"I couldn't leave you lying here." Addie stood, wrapping an arm around his waist to help him stand. He was bigger than her—a lot bigger. But she would do whatever it took to help him. "We need to get you inside."

He blinked, his thoughts seeming to become less hazy. Then his jaw hardened, and he glanced around, probably looking for the person who'd done this to him.

Addie shivered as she remembered the fleeing figure. "He ran to the lake."

Hayes didn't ask any more questions. Not right now, at least.

Instead, Addie grabbed her knife and then helped him into the warm cabin, not letting go of him until they stopped near the crackling fire.

Then she ran back to the door and checked the locks again. For good measure, she shoved a dining room chair beneath the door handle.

That's what people always did on TV. It couldn't hurt now, right?

Wasting no time, she rushed back to Hayes. He stood exactly where she'd left him—near the fire.

She didn't see any blood on him. But he'd have a goose egg on the top of his head soon.

Her stomach knotted as the reality of the situation slammed into her. "Who did this to you?"

"I was hoping you could tell me that." Hayes's haggard gaze caught hers.

She shrugged. She would say Bruce, but he'd left.

"I have no idea," she murmured. "I don't know what's going on."

His gaze—those eyes that at one time Addie had fallen in love with—met hers. "We have a lot to talk about."

Dread pooled in her stomach.

She hoped more than anything Hayes was only referring to what had happened tonight—and that he wasn't referring to their marriage.

Both topics were treacherous.

—————

Hayes's thoughts raced. Of all the things he'd seen himself doing and all the places he'd seen himself going, being here at Lake Tahoe with Addie hadn't been in any of those scenarios.

He was usually much sharper than this. He'd been a Homeland Security agent for more than ten years.

He knew how to handle himself in these kinds of situations.

But he'd let himself get distracted with Addie.

He was lucky to still be alive right now.

"Did something else happen after I talked to you?" He lowered himself onto the edge of an uphol-stered plaid chair.

Addie paced into the kitchen and poured a cup of already-brewed coffee. She shoved it into Hayes's hands, fixed just the way he liked it, and sat across from him.

Addie was still the most gorgeous woman he'd ever laid eyes on.

She always would be.

Her straight dark hair came halfway down her back. A few freckles were scattered across her cheeks. She had a pert nose and warm hazel eyes. Her petite, fit figure made her seem younger than her thirty-three years. She could probably pass for a college student, for that matter.

But would she ever move beyond the demons and pain of her past? Would she truly let down her walls and allow him close?

That's what Hayes wasn't sure about. He'd thought love could conquer all.

But now he wasn't certain.

However, he'd promised to be there for her. Until death do they part.

Addie had refused to let him do that. She'd pushed him away. Claimed she didn't love him anymore.

She'd completely shut him out for four months.

Until now.

"Bruce—Brianna's husband—left." Addie raked a hand through her hair, leaving it tousled on top, as she paced near the fire. "I saw his truck head away from the cabin about an hour ago."

"Did you see Brianna afterward?" He took a sip of his coffee, feeling the warmth seep through him.

Addie shook her head. "I didn't. For all I know, she could've been in the truck. Or she could still be in the cabin. I couldn't see well enough. It was dark, and the cabins are too far apart to make out many details."

Hayes's muscles tightened.

How had Addie walked into the middle of this? She owned an exercise studio and made it her goal in life to bring happiness wherever she went. *Fit people are happy people. A few jumping jacks a day helps to keep the blues away.* Those were her favorite sayings.

Exercise had helped her find her focus.

Exercise and Jesus.

Either way, she wasn't the look-for-crime-around-every-turn type.

Yet trouble always seemed to find her.

Hayes pushed away the memories.

"What are we going to do?" Addie stared at him with wide, round eyes.

When she looked at him like that, Hayes knew she was counting on him to have the answers. To know the next step. To be her hero.

The last thing Hayes wanted to do was to let her down.

He set his coffee on the end table and stood. "I need to go check out your neighbor's cabin."

He stepped toward the door.

As he did, Addie sucked in a breath and grabbed his arm. "I'm not sure that's a good idea."

"I'll be okay."

"Hayes . . ."

As her voice cracked, he looked down at her again and waited for her to finish that statement.

If he wasn't careful, Hayes might think she cared.

Although Addie had made it abundantly clear she didn't. She'd shut the door on their relationship, and for the past month she'd gone as far as to only communicate with him via her attorney.

"Be careful," Addie finally said. "Please."

Hayes stared at her another moment, trying to figure her out.

The task was nearly impossible. She was a puzzle he couldn't solve.

Was that because there were missing pieces? Maybe even pieces that Addie had hidden to ensure he would never get the whole picture?

Finally, Hayes nodded. "I will be."

If only it were possible to keep his heart safe as well.

# CHAPTER
# THREE

ADDIE PACED THE CABIN.

She shouldn't have let Hayes go out there.

Yet she knew she couldn't stop him.

This whole situation felt entirely too dangerous for her liking.

She should have never come here.

There were a lot of things she probably shouldn't have ever done. Was her life just one string of bad decisions? She'd been so determined to rise above the mistakes she'd seen in her mother's life.

Addie had been on track for so long. Had been so hopeful.

Then everything fell apart after her friend Amy died and Addie experienced a home invasion where she'd been held—and hurt—at knifepoint.

Tears rushed to her eyes again.

She walked to the window and peered outside. As she did, Brianna's image filled her mind.

Addie could look at the woman and see in her eyes that something was wrong. That she was scared.

Addie had been there at one time herself. Maybe she was still there . . . but seeing someone else suffer as she had suffered ignited something in her. The sight of it made her feel a rush of courage as she thought about defending someone else the way she hadn't been able to defend herself.

Reggie, her first husband, had almost killed her. Twice.

That was bad enough.

But then there were the other times he'd left her broken and beaten on the floor, feeling like she wanted to die.

Along with that came the emotional abuse.

She'd known she had to get out.

But yet, she'd felt stuck. Immobile.

Three years ago, when she'd heard the news that Reggie had died from a drug overdose, she'd thought she'd found her freedom. But had she really?

Addie shoved those thoughts aside and stared out the window again.

She could vaguely see Hayes at the other cabin. A porch light offered some illumination.

Still, her thoughts raced.

If Bruce wasn't here anymore, then who had hit Hayes over the head?

It didn't make sense.

Were there two separate incidents happening right now?

A rush of coldness filled her veins with such rapid intensity that she began shivering.

As something in her pocket buzzed, Addie jumped.

She scolded herself for the silly reaction.

It was just her phone.

The reception out here was spotty, to put it lightly. Sometimes she had to walk all the way around the cabin until she found a patch where she could get a signal. Other times, it didn't matter what she did, she couldn't call anyone or send any messages.

But it looked as if a text had made it through.

He's going to die.

The breath left her lungs as her head spun.

Was the sender talking about Hayes? Was this text from the same person who'd been threatening her in San Diego? The number was different, but the tone was the same.

The man called himself The Guardian. Whoever

this guy was, he was trying to play God. To control her. To make sure she lived in fear.

Addie didn't have time to figure out the logistics right now.

No, she needed to warn Hayes he was in danger.

———

Hayes walked around the outside of the cabin, careful not to make any sounds—just in case.

The woman—Brianna, Addie had said her name was—could be here. He didn't want to frighten her if she was inside. He simply needed to make sure she was safe and unharmed.

No lights were on. No sounds indicated anyone was stirring. But the woman could be sleeping.

He gripped his gun, his head still pounding.

Hayes hoped Addie was simply overreacting. Given her history, she tended to see these situations differently than other people.

But that didn't mean she was paranoid. He had no doubt some type of conflict had occurred over here.

Hayes just didn't know if it was a marital spat or if there was more to it.

Hopefully, he could find out and then Addie could sleep a little better.

Whatever happened, he needed to convince her to go back to San Diego. Her being out here alone was a terrible idea. If something happened to her, no one would even hear her scream, nor could she call for help.

As he continued around the neighboring cabin, he remained on guard. No one was going to take him by surprise again.

He thought the person who'd hit him over the head was long gone. But Hayes couldn't take any chances.

When he saw nothing outside, he went to the front door and knocked.

As he did, the hinges creaked.

His breath caught.

The lock wasn't latched.

Strange. Most people who spent time out here knew to keep their doors secured and shut. Wildlife was abundant in the area, and a bear could easily come inside this place looking for food if given the opportunity.

Hayes's shoulders tightened.

He pushed the door open and peered inside. "Hello?"

Silence filled the air.

He pushed the door farther open and stepped inside. "Anyone here?"

Still no answer.

He'd guess the place was empty. But he needed to be certain.

He turned on his flashlight and shone it around the space.

Moving quickly, he checked the small cabin for any signs of life.

There were none.

He wasn't sure if that would make Addie feel better or worse.

When Bruce had left, he must have taken Brianna with him. Perhaps against her wishes. Or maybe she'd gone willingly. It was hard to say without more information.

As far as Hayes could see, there were no signs of foul play.

Trying to be thorough, he shone his flashlight around the place one more time, looking for any fine details.

On the table by the couch was a map of the lake and a roll of duct tape.

He paused.

Duct tape? That didn't necessarily mean anything criminal. But the tape was torn, the end of it sticking out from the rest of the roll. It had been used recently.

Hayes stored that fact in the back of his mind.

Then he checked the rest of the living room before wandering into the small kitchen.

When his light hit the kitchen counter, he stopped in his tracks.

Some onions were chopped and left on a cutting board. A pan sat on the stove, oil glazing the bottom. He held his hand over the pot. It was cold. No stove lights were on.

Still, it almost looked as if someone had started to cook and had stopped unexpectedly.

His light touched on something else.

Four drops of blood dotted the butcher block top.

His heart rate quickened.

Maybe Addie had been right. Maybe something *had* happened here.

Suddenly, he wasn't comfortable being this far away from her.

As he turned to head outside, a creak sounded behind him.

And he knew someone else was here.

# CHAPTER
# FOUR

ADDIE RAN AS if she were being chased.

Even though she wasn't.

Still, fear pulsed inside her. Her thoughts felt as frantic as her emotions. As her breathing.

Something bad was going to happen.

And she had to warn Hayes.

She couldn't let anyone hurt him.

She reached Brianna's cabin. Operating on pure adrenaline, she darted up the steps to the porch.

When she saw the door was open, she skidded to a halt.

Something could have already happened to Hayes. What if The Guardian was here with him? If the man had followed her here, determined to keep his deadly promises?

She froze as fear consumed her.

But she couldn't just stand here on the porch.

*You have to do something!*

She supposed she could call the police if she could find a signal.

But the thought of running back across the open expanse between the cabins also terrified her.

*Don't panic now*, Addie told herself. *Stay strong. You can do this.*

She glanced over her shoulder. Didn't see anyone.

Yet she could feel a panic attack coming on.

She was so messed up. She'd thought she'd been doing better.

Clearly, she wasn't.

Her throat tightened, and tension squeezed her entire body.

She remembered what she'd learned in counseling.

She took a step inside and named three things she could see—the logs comprising the wall, the generic light switch, the plaid curtain over the window. Identified three sounds—birds squawking outside, the clock ticking on the wall, the refrigerator humming. Moved three body parts—her fingers as they gripped the door, her feet as she shuffled forward, her lips as they rubbed together.

Those things helped to ground her, but she had no time to repeat the steps again.

Not when Hayes could be in trouble.

Addie drew in a deep breath as she gathered her courage.

She would check this place out. She had no choice at this point.

Forcing her feet to move, she stepped farther inside the cabin and then listened.

She didn't hear anyone moving.

Where was Hayes? Should she call for him? Or would that just alert someone else—possibly someone dangerous—that she was here?

She didn't have Hayes's instincts. Instead, she constantly second-guessed herself.

Her counselor said it was due to the years of abuse she'd endured with Reggie.

Regardless, she wasn't going to back out now.

As she stepped toward the small hallway in the distance, she sensed movement behind her.

Heard a footstep.

Felt the disturbance in the air.

Before she could react, a muscular arm encircled her neck.

And Addie knew she was going to die.

———

"Addie?" Hayes released his grip as he stared at his wife.

"Hayes?" She spun around and nearly collapsed in front of him.

He caught her elbow, holding her up.

Then he stared at her in confusion. "I asked you to stay at the cabin."

"I know, but I thought you were . . ." Her voice cracked as she stared up at him, emotions pooling in her eyes. "I was worried. Scared."

He set aside his irritation when he saw the fear on her face. "Addie . . . you could've gotten hurt. I thought you were an intruder."

"I didn't mean to distract you." Addie scanned the place, her expression pensive. "Did you find her? Is Brianna here?"

"No one is here."

Addie blew out a breath. "I just don't know what to think."

As Hayes stared at Addie, he had the urge to pull her into his arms. To tell her that everything would be okay.

But that was no longer his right. Nor would the motion be welcome.

She'd made that clear.

However, it took every ounce of his self-control not to reach for her. To give in to his instincts.

But she'd asked for space, and that's what Hayes needed to give her. Reggie had stalked and tormented Addie after she'd left him. Hayes didn't want to be that guy. There was a fine line between persistence and intimidation.

"Any signs of foul play?" Her eyes roamed the place as she shivered.

He considered what to tell her. If he mentioned the duct tape and blood, Addie would be beside herself.

But he didn't want to lie either.

Instead, he directed her toward the door. "Let's get back to the cabin. We'll talk there."

Addie didn't argue.

She also didn't resist Hayes's touch as he kept a hand on her arm and led her back toward her place.

The wind—cold and sharp—blew over them, bringing with it the crisp scent of pine trees and Addie's soft cotton perfume. Hayes had always loved that smell.

But he couldn't relish it too much. Not now.

In fact, he needed to get those sweet memories out of his system because Addie had made herself clear.

They were over.

Yet Hayes still wasn't ready to walk away. He'd

prayed about what to do, and he sensed a silent urge to stay.

He glanced around as they walked, looking for a sign of anyone who might be lurking nearby.

He saw nothing and no one.

But everything about this situation had him on edge.

As soon as they got back to Addie's cabin, he locked the door behind them and then turned toward her.

They needed to talk.

But as Addie looked up at him, something flashed through her gaze.

Was that . . . guilt?

"There's something I should tell you." She nibbled on her lip before holding up her phone. "I got this text while you were over here."

Hayes took the phone from her and read the message. *He's going to die.*

Alarm rushed through him.

Whatever was going on here, he didn't like it.

ADDIE FELT the trembles overtake her.

She *hated* this whole situation.

She almost hadn't shown Hayes that text. But he'd come here and put his life at risk. She couldn't stay quiet forever about what had happened.

Yet she feared he'd ask too many questions.

He deserved all the answers.

But Addie wasn't in a place right now where she could give them. She was trying to do the right thing, yet the right thing felt so hard.

She knew this guy had killed Amy. He wouldn't hesitate to kill Hayes too.

He was sneaky. Addie could ask Hayes for help, but it wouldn't do any good. The best thing she'd been able to do was listen to this guy's directions and obey him.

She rubbed her throat as she tried to pull herself together. "You said you didn't see anything inside the cabin? So, it looks like Bruce took Brianna with him when he left. They only had the one vehicle."

Something flickered in Hayes's eyes. "We can only assume."

Addie twisted her head, hearing the strange undertone to his voice. "What does that mean?"

He let out a long breath and stared in the distance as if he didn't want to answer. But Addie knew Hayes well enough to recognize that look. For some reason, he didn't want to tell her something.

She needed to know what was going on. This was no time to conceal the truth in order to protect her. However, Addie knew she had no room to talk when it came to holding back the truth.

Doing so had defined her life for the past several months.

"Hayes?" She stared at him, waiting for him to make eye contact.

He let out a sigh as their gazes met. "If you must know, I saw some duct tape and a few drops of blood inside Brianna's cabin."

Addie sucked in a breath. "What?"

Duct tape didn't necessarily mean anything.

But blood . . .

Her head began to swim with possibilities. Terrible, terrible possibilities.

Memories hit her.

Memories of the pain she'd endured. Of the bruises Reggie had left. The bones he'd broken. She'd even lost a tooth.

"Addie . . ." He squeezed her arm, his touch bringing her back to her current reality.

"Tell me about the . . . blood," Addie started. "How much was there? Where was it?"

Hayes rubbed his jaw. "I saw four drops of blood on the counter near the kitchen sink. Someone also left some onions out, diced as if they were about to cook. Brianna or Bruce could have cut themselves while slicing up vegetables for dinner, for all I know. There wasn't enough blood to truly be concerned. But given everything you've told me . . ."

"We need to tell the police," Addie finished.

Hayes rubbed his jaw, which looked hardened with determination. "Right now, I'm more concerned about getting you out of here. Grab your things. I'm going to drive you somewhere else. This place clearly isn't safe."

"But . . ." Addie didn't want to tell Hayes her real reasons for coming here.

Then he'd know something was up. Then she'd

have to tell him the truth about everything that had happened.

He'd done so much for her.

Now it was her turn to protect him.

However, it might be too late. Hayes was here.

Addie had disobeyed the demands forced upon her. She knew what the consequences would be.

"We can talk more later." Hayes's deep voice cut into her thoughts. "But for tonight, we shouldn't stay here."

Finally, Addie nodded.

She thought through all she'd need to pack.

She didn't care about the food she'd brought. The property manager could toss that later or take it home.

That left her clothes and toiletry items.

She grabbed her suitcase, tossed everything inside, and walked back into the living room.

Hayes stood in the middle of the space, his hands on his hips, appearing in cop mode. The ashes in the fireplace smoked as if he'd just put out the flames.

"I'm going to drive you tonight." His voice left no room for argument as he took the suitcase from her. "We can come back for your car later."

That sounded perfect because Addie didn't think she could handle herself behind the wheel right now.

Hayes led her outside, his hand skimming her lower back.

She'd always loved it when he placed his hand there. She felt so protected. So cherished.

There weren't many times in her life that Addie had felt cherished and loved unconditionally. But with Hayes, she always had.

But those were feelings she needed to squash. The two of them could never be together again.

She had to remember that, even if her heart ached at the thought.

They stepped around to the other side of the cabin to where the vehicles were parked.

As they did, both Hayes and Addie stopped in their tracks.

They wouldn't be going anywhere.

Their tires had all been slashed.

———

As soon as Hayes saw the flattened wheels of his SUV, he tensed.

He dropped Addie's suitcase.

With one hand, he grabbed his gun. With the other, he slid Addie behind him.

He glanced around, searching for the person

who'd done this. The person who'd essentially trapped them here at this cabin miles away from civilization.

Someone had disabled their vehicles while Hayes and Addie were at the neighboring cabin. It was the only block of time that made sense.

That meant this person could still be close.

Possibly even watching right now. Targeting them. Waiting to strike.

Tension threaded between Hayes's shoulder blades. "We need to get back inside. Now."

Addie's breath caught as she stood behind him, but she said nothing.

With one more glance around the area, he grabbed Addie's suitcase and quickly escorted her back into the cabin.

Once he was sure everything was secure, he placed his gun back into his holster.

But there was no way he could sit down and relax. They had to figure out what to do next.

He pulled out his phone and frowned.

Still no signal.

He'd been trying to find one since he arrived. Clearly, there was reception *sometimes*. Addie had called him from the cabin. But it was spotty at best.

He glanced at Addie as she sank into an armchair

near the fireplace, her eyes glazed and her motions jittery with anxiety.

He knew about her struggles.

They'd never bothered him. Well, they bothered him—but only in the sense that he wanted to see her get better. And she *had* been doing so much better.

He wasn't sure what it was about that home invasion that had changed everything. He'd feared maybe she'd been sexually assaulted, but Addie had assured him she wasn't.

Yet that incident had transformed her into a different person. She'd never opened up about exactly what happened. Had refused to talk to him about it.

That made him feel like such a failure . . . his own wife didn't trust him enough to tell him the truth.

A familiar ache returned to his chest.

The only thing he could figure was that the trauma had triggered something inside her—something she still hadn't moved beyond.

"Is there anything you need to tell me?" Hayes stepped closer to her, his muscles still poised to act if necessary.

Addie shook her head, that forlorn look still in her eyes as she rubbed her arms. "I don't know what you want me to say."

Hayes tried to hold back any judgment, to not

push her too hard. But he was in the dark right now, and he didn't like it. "What about the text? Do you know who sent it?"

She opened her mouth but shut it again.

Then another thought slammed into Hayes's mind.

He'd been assuming that text was about him.

But what if Addie already had someone else in her life? What if that was secretly what their breakup had been about? Had she come to this place to meet with her boyfriend?

He swallowed the surge of jealousy that rushed through him.

Before he'd met Addie, he'd been engaged. His fiancée had cheated on him with one of his friends.

Addie knew how devastated he'd been at the betrayal. He hadn't seen her as the type to do something like that.

Was he wrong?

He didn't want to ask the question, but he had to know. "Addie . . . is that text about me or are you seeing someone else?"

Her eyes widened with surprise at his question. "No . . . I'm not seeing anyone else. Our divorce isn't even final."

Her proclamation made Hayes feel a little better.

But as Hayes studied her face, he realized there was more to this.

Somehow, he was going to have to convince Addie to share whatever information she knew.

Especially since it could be connected with the danger surrounding them now.

ADDIE COULDN'T TELL Hayes the truth.

More than anything, she wanted to spill everything.

But she had to remain quiet now—for the same reasons she had to remain quiet about why she left him four months ago.

She knew exactly what Hayes would do if he knew the details of the home invasion.

He'd get himself killed.

She loved Hayes too much to let that happen. He might not ever believe she still cared about him—and she couldn't blame him for that. But it was true. Someone else—someone twisted and methodical—was calling the shots. She was simply a puppet at his mercy.

But The Guardian seemed to know her every

move. Seemed to know every time she even thought about calling Hayes.

He'd explained it to her in detail. Maybe it would be a car bomb beneath Hayes's vehicle. Maybe it would be a random shooting that no one could explain. Maybe it would be poison. The Guardian claimed he had a lot of tricks up his sleeve, and Addie believed him.

After several minutes of silence, Addie finally asked, "What are we going to do?"

It seemed safer to stick with their physical security right now than it did to talk about their hearts.

Hayes glanced at his phone again before rubbing his jaw. "We have no cell service. There's no landline. Neither of our vehicles are drivable. I'd say we don't have much choice but to hunker down for the night."

"The cabin has hardwired internet, in case that helps."

"Good to know. But it won't be much help now."

Addie nodded. She figured he'd say that. There weren't many alternatives out here in the middle of nowhere.

Hayes let out a sigh and glanced around again. "Are there any other neighbors nearby who could help?"

"Just Brianna and Bruce. The next cabin is probably a half a mile away, and I'm not sure it's occupied. Most in this area aren't at this time of year."

He nodded solemnly. "That makes sense. When did Bruce and Brianna get here?"

"Early this morning."

"And when did you arrive?"

"Yesterday afternoon."

He seemed to process that as he nodded. "Okay. We'll wait until the morning to do anything. I don't want to be out there when it's dark. It's too easy for someone to hide and ambush us. You can get some sleep, and I'll keep watch."

Addie's throat tightened as Hayes took charge of the situation—as he instinctively took care of her. He was always so good at doing that.

"I don't want you to stay awake all night . . ." she murmured as she sat there staring at him.

Hayes offered a tight shrug. "I can't sleep knowing someone is out there who might want to harm you."

Addie opened her mouth, wanting to argue with his statement.

But she couldn't.

Hayes was that type of guy. He was vigilant. Of course, he'd stay up all night to make sure nothing happened.

Without asking, he grabbed some kindling and

began to start another fire. There was a definite chill in the air, and some warmth sounded really nice.

Just thinking about it made her rub her arms as goosebumps spread across her skin.

She shifted in the chair. "I can't believe you got here so fast. I figured you would just give me advice over the phone."

He shrugged as he continued adding wood to the fireplace. "I just finished up an assignment in Reno. I had no idea you were so close."

"An assignment?" Addie had been curious about his life since their split. But she hadn't felt as if it was her right to ask.

"I work for an organization in Arizona called Vanishing Ranch." He shifted, looking more comfortable at the subject change. Then he grabbed a lighter and aimed it at the kindling below the logs.

"What is that? What do you do for them?" She scooted back in the chair and pulled her knees to her chest.

"It's a horse rescue, officially. But we also help women—and sometimes men—who need to get out of difficult situations. We set them up with new identities and places to live if that's what they want. But mostly, we try to make sure that innocent people in hard situations have every resource they need to stay safe."

Emotion—possibly gratitude—clutched her. Addie had to wonder if Hayes had taken that job because of her . . . because of her past.

But she didn't dare ask. Didn't dare open those floodgates.

Instead, she said, "That sounds like a worthy organization."

He shrugged, his expression not giving away too much. "I think so."

Addie wanted to say more, but she wasn't sure what. She hated the awkwardness between them—especially considering how wonderful their years together had been.

But everything had changed . . .

She sat silently for several minutes, watching as the flames grew higher. Fires had always mesmerized her.

Hayes sat on the couch, also staring silently at the blaze.

After several minutes of quiet, Addie licked her lips, feeling the urge to say something.

But what?

She was afraid if she started talking, she'd open up to him completely. She couldn't do that.

Instead, she yawned and rose. "I should probably go to bed. It's been a long day."

"Probably a good idea."

As she took a step toward the hallway, she paused and glanced back at Hayes.

Her throat tightened when she saw his broad frame. His warm eyes. His confident movements. "Hayes . . . thank you."

He stared at her a moment, something unreadable in his eyes. "Of course."

At once, she had a flashback of their marriage. Of the warm nights they'd spent together. Of cuddling on cold mornings. Of sharing kisses and affection.

Now that was all over.

She couldn't forget that fact.

———

Addie lay in bed unable to sleep, even though she knew it was the middle of the night.

She wasn't sure the cause of her restlessness. Was she listening for the sound of an intruder? Or was it because Hayes was here with her?

Maybe it was both.

As she pressed her head into her pillow, Hayes's image filled her mind.

Her heart warmed as she remembered the way he used to look at her.

Hayes had been the best thing to ever happen to her.

But as her mom had always told her, if there was one thing Addie was skilled at doing, it was ruining anything good in her life.

That prophecy, spoken over her from a young age, seemed to have proven true.

Addie punched her pillow and stuffed it under her head, trying to erase the bad memories of her challenging upbringing.

But the task felt impossible.

Things had started falling apart for her beginning with what had happened to her baby brother, Chip.

It had been her job to protect him. But while Addie had been watching him when he was six and she was twelve, he'd chased a ball into the road. She'd called for him. Yelled for him to stop.

He didn't.

A car had hit him, killing him on scene.

Everything had gone downhill after that.

Her mom had turned to drugs to cope and had transformed into a different person. She'd blamed Addie for what had happened.

Addie blamed herself. She should have been paying more attention.

Chip had died because of her, and Addie had never forgiven herself for it.

As soon as Addie was old enough, she'd gotten

out of the house. She hadn't had money to go to college, so she'd begun working at a gym.

That's where she'd met Reggie, a construction worker.

He'd been charming at first. Kind and thoughtful. Attentive. Handsome.

When Reggie had proposed, marriage had seemed like a way out, an answer to her problems. Addie had truly cared about Reggie, and she'd thought he'd loved her in return.

Only a couple of months into their marriage, Addie had realized Reggie's behavior had all been an act. But it was too late. She was in too deep.

The abuse had begun with occasional demeaning comments. Gaslighting. Subtle putdowns that eventually turned into outright cruelty.

He'd started gripping her arm too hard.

Pushing her.

The first time he'd smacked her across the face, she'd been stunned.

He'd apologized. Said it wouldn't ever happen again.

Then it did.

And it got worse.

The more control he gained, the more he wanted.

Eventually, he'd almost killed her.

After suffering through their marriage for eight

years, Addie finally found the strength to leave him. Thankfully, they'd had no kids.

Addie had wanted a family, but Reggie didn't. At one time, she'd dreamed about the family she and Hayes might one day have. That dream had also died.

She pressed her eyes closed, wishing she could shut out her memories.

Except for the memories of when she'd met Hayes.

He was truly the best thing that had ever happened to her.

Maybe she shouldn't have called him tonight. If she hadn't, then he wouldn't be in danger right now.

She reflected on what Hayes had told her about his new job. He was helping women in abusive situations get a new start.

Had he taken that job because of her? Had he taken this position because he'd seen firsthand how devastating abusive relationships could be?

There had to be a connection.

Her affection for Hayes grew even deeper.

If only she could act on it.

Her lungs froze as she heard a scratching noise outside her window.

Was someone here? Had The Guardian found her?

Was this person trying to get inside?

She wanted to turn to see.

But she felt numb.

Frozen.

She couldn't move.

*Yes, you can,* she told herself. *You're stronger than your fears.*

If someone was out there, she needed to know.

Bracing herself, Addie took several deep breaths before finally shifting in her bed to look.

She didn't want to be the girl who cried wolf. So she'd check first.

But she hoped she wouldn't regret this.

# CHAPTER
# SEVEN

HAYES HAD BEEN PACING the cabin for most of the night. Peering out the windows. Looking for signs of anything suspicious.

Everything outside seemed quiet.

But he didn't like this situation.

Still, he was thankful Addie had at least called him. The fact she'd reached out seemed like a step in the right direction. He hadn't given up on their marriage.

What they had was too special. Their connection ran too deep.

Hayes had prayed ever since Addie left him that they'd have the opportunity to reconcile. That Addie would open up to him. That she would trust him with the secrets she harbored in her heart.

But she'd seemed totally closed to that possibility.

Addie asking Hayes for help didn't necessarily change that. But at least it gave him a spark of hope.

He glanced at his phone again, hoping to find a signal so he could call either the police or his colleagues at Vanishing Ranch. Someone else needed to know what was going on—just in case. At least the internet was hardwired. He could email someone if necessary.

If Hayes were the only one involved, he would walk down the road until he found a signal so he could get out of here tonight.

But he knew Addie would insist on going with him, and he couldn't chance her getting hurt. They were safer behind these four walls—for now.

He let out a breath and glanced around the cozy log cabin with its stone fireplace, rich colors, and stunning views.

Lake Tahoe stretched in the distance, glimmering under the moonlight.

After they'd gotten married, Addie had often talked about wanting to come here. They'd even mentioned having a second honeymoon here one day.

Then Addie had opened her exercise studio, which had consumed most of her time. Hayes had been caught up in his job with Homeland Security.

But he'd thought they were making their schedules work. When they were tired, they were tired. But when they played hard, they played hard. They'd hiked together, explored small towns, and eaten at hole-in-the-wall restaurants.

They'd had a great time together.

But everything had seemed to change in an instant.

Well, not really an instant.

The home invasion had lasted over an hour. Hayes had been working a job across the country.

But Addie had been home. He would have blamed Reggie for the crime, but Addie's ex-husband was dead. The perpetrator appeared to be someone random.

From what Hayes understood, the intruder had roughed Addie up before stealing some jewelry and all the cash they'd set aside for vacation.

After that day, she'd started to withdraw.

Addie had told him she felt uneasy being home alone so often, but he'd never thought things would happen the way they did.

Hayes had blamed himself for not being there.

Then one day, a week after the break-in, Addie had told him she didn't love him and didn't want to be married anymore. She'd asked him to leave.

When he'd asked for more details, Addie had

simply told him she preferred the single life. One where she was unattached.

Hayes couldn't help but think her change of heart was because he hadn't been there when she needed him.

The two of them had met when Hayes showed up for her kickboxing class at the gym where she worked. He'd later admitted that he'd seen her while he was lifting weights and had decided to take her class in hopes of having an excuse to talk to her.

They'd gone out three days later. Six months afterward, they married.

The days Hayes had shared with her had been some of the best of his life.

Until it had all fallen apart.

In an effort to reconcile, Hayes had stepped away from his job with Homeland Security, thinking if he did something less demanding that maybe they could work things out. He *had* traveled a lot. Maybe that had taken a toll on their relationship. Maybe that had bothered Addie more than she admitted, and she hadn't wanted to say anything.

But Addie still wanted nothing to do with him, even after he'd quit.

Finally, he'd taken the job at Vanishing Ranch. His boss, Charlie Soldier, knew he needed a flexible schedule. It was one of the reasons he'd wanted to work there. If he needed to get away and help Addie, he could.

But he'd never expected to get a frantic call from her. Not like this.

He let out a sigh and lowered himself onto the brown leather couch near the fireplace. He didn't want to get too comfortable, but maybe he could relax a moment.

As he leaned back, he remembered the text Addie received earlier. *He's going to die.*

Hayes still had to wonder if the texter had been referring to someone else. Another man in Addie's life.

But the thought of Addie being with anyone else . . . it tore him up inside.

Addie would never do that . . . right?

As she'd said, their divorce wasn't final.

If he had anything to say about it, it never would be.

Hayes ran a hand over his face as he tried to keep a tight rein on his emotions.

Nothing made sense.

First thing in the morning, Hayes would find a way to contact the police. He and Addie couldn't stay here indefinitely. They needed to have their tires replaced. To report the incident at the other cabin.

Just then, the lights above him flickered before going out.

His spine went rigid.

Had someone cut the power? Or had the raging wind outside done this?

He frowned as he went to the window and peered out. But he didn't see anything or anyone.

Thankfully, the fire warmed the room. But he had other concerns.

A thump sounded in the distance.

He reached for his gun.

The sound had come from the direction of Addie's room.

He darted toward her door.

Just as he reached it, it opened. Addie stood there with a sheepish expression on her face.

The sight of her with her disheveled hair and sleepy eyes took his breath away. Took him back in time.

"Sorry—I thought I heard something outside," she said. "I accidentally knocked a book onto the floor when I got up to check it out. But it was only a branch scraping the window."

He released the air from his lungs. "I'm glad you're okay."

"Sorry to concern you."

"By the way, the power is out," he told her. "You

might need some extra blankets. The fireplace is the only thing lighting up this place right now."

Her eyebrows shot up. "The power?"

"I think it was the wind, but I'll keep my eyes open for any signs of trouble."

"I know you will." She almost sounded wistful as she said the words.

Before stepping away, he looked out the window at the utter darkness outside.

For now, all Hayes could do was stay vigilant until daylight.

———

Addie awoke with a start and glanced around.

Early morning sunlight streamed through her window as she sat up and her blanket tumbled to her waist.

She'd been asleep.

She'd *actually* fallen asleep. She'd thought for sure she'd be up all night.

Her lost hours brought her a moment of panic.

What if something bad had happened during the night and she'd slept through it? She hadn't slept well for the past four months. But last night . . . she must have been sleeping like the proverbial log.

That was despite everything that had happened.

Was it because Hayes was here?

Probably, but Addie couldn't allow herself to think about that now.

Quickly, she climbed out of bed, opened her door, and peered out.

Hayes was wide awake, sitting on the couch, and staring at the fire he'd kept going through the night. He sipped on a cup of coffee, its rich scent mingling with the woodsy aroma of the fire.

Coffee?

That must mean the power was back on.

Relief filled her.

She remained where she was a moment and stared at Hayes.

He looked just as handsome as ever in his jeans and flannel shirt.

Six months ago, Addie would have stepped behind him and wrapped her arms around his neck before planting a kiss on his cheek. He would have taken her hand, pulled her around in front of him, and folded her into his arms.

The memories of those sweet moments caused an ache to form in her chest.

As Addie rubbed her eyes, she noticed the moisture there.

Tears were the last thing she needed. She'd cried enough of those to last a lifetime.

Instead, she quietly went back into her room, did some morning stretches, and then got ready for the day. When she emerged again, the scent of bacon filled the air.

Hayes stood at the stove, flipping pancakes and frying strips of bacon.

Addie folded her arms across her chest as she paced toward him.

As she did, Hayes glanced up and offered a tight smile. "Morning. I thought I'd fix your favorite meal of the day."

"It smells wonderful." Addie sat on a barstool at the island and watched as he finished cooking.

A moment later, he placed a plate in front of her. Bacon, eggs, and pancakes.

Addie had forgotten how much she enjoyed having other people take care of her on occasion.

Hayes in particular.

Doing life with someone you loved was so much better than doing life alone.

But sometimes circumstances dictated what happened to you, not the other way around. She'd struggled with that fact for a long time until she'd finally come to accept it. Addie wished she could proclaim she had more peace in her life since then, but she didn't.

"How did you sleep?" Hayes placed another

piece of bacon on a plate before turning off the burner.

"All things considered, I guess I did okay. You?"

"I didn't sleep." He shrugged. "I wasn't comfortable resting, not after everything that happened."

"You're going to be tired." Addie gave him a knowing look.

After all, who took care of the person who took care of everyone else? She'd claimed the position once. But no more.

"I'm used to not getting sleep," he murmured. "Comes with the territory."

Addie knew he told the truth. Hayes's schedule had been totally messed up when he'd worked for Homeland Security. She, on the other hand, was the type who thrived on routine. There was no way she could have ever done his job.

"You're not eating?" She nodded toward the empty counter in front of him.

"I've been munching on some bacon as I cooked. I'll be fine."

Addie nodded before closing her eyes and lifting a quick prayer. *Thank You, Father, for the food. Thank You for Hayes being here as well. I'm sorry . . . well, for everything.*

She almost felt guilty praying the prayer. Almost felt guilty talking to God at all.

She knew what God thought about divorce. It wasn't something she took lightly.

She mourned for so much—for things she couldn't express or put into words.

Somehow, she had to make things right. But she wasn't sure how.

Even if she didn't want to admit it, Hayes's presence right now was an answer to prayer. A big one. Could God possibly still love her despite her failings? Could He still be watching out for her, even in the midst of her failures?

Her upbringing would tell her no. Would tell her that love had a direct correlation to worthiness. But Hayes had always told her God's love didn't work like that. That He loved unconditionally.

She still had a hard time processing—and truly believing—that.

When she opened her eyes, she saw Hayes studying her.

She quickly looked away.

Addie knew he must hate her. She couldn't blame him.

However, Addie hadn't had much other choice. If she stayed with him, then Hayes would be killed. That had become abundantly clear through an endless stream of text messages and pictures someone had sent.

Those weren't idle threats.

The person terrorizing her wanted to make it clear he was watching. Waiting. Anticipating.

But would Hayes even believe Addie if she told him the truth? Or was it too late for them to make things right?

It didn't matter. Telling him the truth was too risky.

With Hayes's life on the line, it wasn't a chance she could take.

# CHAPTER
# EIGHT

HAYES TOOK another sip of his coffee as he watched Addie dig into her breakfast.

He wished circumstances were different. That the two of them were simply here to talk about their relationship. To work through it. To come up with a solution.

But their marriage appeared to be the elephant in the room—the very thing Addie didn't want to discuss.

At the same time, Hayes simply had to focus on keeping Addie safe. That was his top priority at the moment. He did it for perfect strangers who were in dangerous situations. Of course, he'd do it for his wife as well.

As Hayes began to wipe some splatters of grease

from around the griddle, Addie looked up at him with questions in her gaze. "Do we have a plan?"

He continued to wipe the counter. "I'm going to need to walk up the road until I find a cell signal so I can call someone for help."

Her eyes widened as she paused with a fork in midair. "That doesn't seem safe. Whoever knocked you out, who slashed our tires . . . they could still be close."

He shrugged. "It's really the only option right now."

"I can't stay here alone." Her voice tightened with fear. "Please, don't try to make me."

Hayes stared at her, unable to ignore the fear in her tone.

She was terrified, wasn't she?

She had to be if she'd called him for help.

Finally, he nodded, his mind made up. "We can walk together if that will make you feel better. We'll just need to be careful."

Her shoulders seemed to slump with relief. "Okay. Yes, that sounds good. When?"

He nodded to the window, now lined with an icy white trim. "It snowed quite a bit last night. We probably need to wait until the sun comes up more. Do you have any snow gear with you? Did the owners leave a snowmobile?"

"No snowmobile." Addie frowned. "I have . . . a few things. I didn't exactly plan on being out there making a snowman or anything. You?"

"I brought some winter gear, just in case." If there was one thing he was, it was always prepared. Plus, he still had some things in his bag leftover from an assignment he had in Aspen not long ago.

Addie took another bite of her bacon.

Hayes had always loved all her little quirks. How she was a health-food nut but loved bacon and sugary lattes. How she picked through her lettuce, making sure every piece was perfectly green with no bitter stalks. She could make a killer salad because of that. How when she got stressed, she either exercised or baked.

But he couldn't let himself get caught up in those memories.

Instead, he leveled his gaze with hers. "Why are you really here, Addie?"

Her face paled, and she pushed her plate away as if she'd suddenly lost her appetite. At least, she'd already eaten half of her food.

As she opened her mouth to speak, Hayes braced himself for whatever truth she was about to share.

———

Addie licked her lips.

She'd figured that question would come up. Last night before she went to bed, she'd thought about how to answer.

Hayes could read her so easily. He'd always been like that. It was like he knew her better than she knew herself. She'd never met someone who understood her so well before.

Sometimes, the fact was almost unnerving.

Finally, after several seconds of thought, she shrugged. "I just needed to get away."

Hayes narrowed his eyes, leaving no doubt he was analyzing the situation—and her answer. "Who's running your studio?"

"Danielle. I've hired a few more people to help me over the past couple of months." Danielle was another fitness instructor and one of Addie's closest friends.

"It sounds like the studio is doing well."

She glanced at her eggs as they grew cold. "It's growing more and more. All that hard work has paid off."

Hayes had been such a big support when she'd opened Pinnacle Fitness. It was a smaller studio, but she offered several exercise classes a day. So far, the business was paying for itself and even turning a small profit.

"That's great news. But why are you here?" He leaned toward her with his palms on the counter, his laser-like gaze on her. "I know there's got to be more to the story."

Addie knew one thing: she'd never want to be sitting across an interrogation table from him. "You know I've always wanted to come here."

"But alone?" He glanced around. "This place is secluded. Did you even tell anyone where you were?"

She heard the accusation in his voice. Or was that worry? She couldn't be sure.

Maybe the accusation was actually internal, her own guilt speaking.

Addie wanted to deny his words, but she knew Hayes would see through her. "My friends are letting me use their place, so they know. Otherwise, I just wanted some privacy."

A new emotion passed through his gaze. "Were you coming here to meet someone?"

Her eyebrows shot up. "What? No . . . I came here to be alone."

How could Hayes think that? It was the second time he'd implied as much. But given the way Addie ended things, could she really blame him? Probably not.

In fact, he probably thought that's why she called

things off—because she'd met someone else. Nothing could be further from the truth.

She knew how heartbroken Hayes had been when his fiancée had cheated on him. She'd never do that to him. Never.

He stared at her another moment, questions brewing in his gaze.

Before he could ask them, Addie stood. "I'm going to grab my coat. Probably the sooner we start walking, the better. Right?"

Even though he'd said earlier that they needed to wait, Addie didn't think she could just sit here any longer. She needed to do something.

Finally, Hayes nodded. "That's fine. I'll get cleaned up, and then we'll head out. Maybe we'll run into someone who has cell service. Otherwise, we can walk until we find some. I don't know how long that will take."

She didn't either. But she was ready to get busy.

Addie wasn't sure if it was this situation that had her spooked or if having Hayes here with her had left her feeling overwhelmed.

Either way, she needed some fresh air.

# CHAPTER
# NINE

AS SOON AS Hayes stepped from the cabin, he surveyed the landscape around him.

The snow was the perfect canvas to display any potential evidence.

He searched the ground.

Some prints left by a deer caught his eye, but nothing else.

He glanced back at Addie, who waited in the doorway behind him. "Are you sure you're ready for this?"

She pulled her cheerful teal hat down over her ears and nodded. But her nose was already red, as were her cheeks. "I can do this."

It was twenty-three degrees outside according to a thermometer at the cabin. Walking should help keep them warm, but it wouldn't be easy—it wasn't as if they'd be traversing a flat road. These roads wound around the mountainside.

Before they started their trek, Hayes glanced at the lake.

The turquoise waters matched Addie's hat, and the white snow hugging the edges of the lake made the place almost look magical. He knew why people loved coming here.

It was another gorgeous display of God's handiwork.

As was Addie—both on the inside and out. But would she ever realize that? Would she ever truly know her worth? That diamonds and rubies had nothing on her?

"Are you ready?" Addie's voice pulled him from his thoughts.

He turned toward her and nodded. "Yes, let's go."

With phones tucked in their pockets, they started up the road. Ponderosa pine, junipers, and even a grove of aspens stood watch around them. Their branches were covered with snow that rained down below whenever the wind blew.

The trees stretched between the road and the lake. Hayes knew that treacherous cliffs waited where the mountain met the water. He'd seen the craggy drop-offs from the shore near Addie's cabin. In front of her place, it was sandy and flat. But as the landscape changed, it became more dangerous.

The peaceful scenery around them was such a stark contrast to the reality of their current situation—both the danger at the cabin and the brokenness between them.

Hayes paused as he heard a vehicle coming their way. Taking Addie's arm, he led her to the side of the road. The snow made it icy and slick. The last thing they needed was to be in the path of a vehicle that lost control.

As the truck came closer, Addie gasped and clutched his arm.

His muscles stiffened. "What is it?"

"That's Bruce's truck . . ."

———

Addie could hardly breathe as the rundown cobalt blue truck came to a stop beside them.

A moment later, the driver leaned over the seat and rolled down the passenger side window.

It was him. Bruce.

Just as Addie had thought.

Tension threaded her chest at the sight of him. The man was probably in his early thirties, with ruddy skin and coarse blond hair. The hair atop his head was the same length as the hair on his cheeks, upper lip, and eyebrows. The man had a thick neck, a barrel-like belly, and a bulbous nose.

"Everything okay out here?" Bruce peered out at them, his expression friendly enough.

Hayes wrapped an arm around Addie's waist and pulled her a little closer. "We're fine. Just taking in the sights and sounds around us."

Addie's lungs froze at Hayes's touch. She'd missed it so much. But she couldn't let her mind go there, no matter how tempting.

Hayes was only acting affectionate with her right now so Bruce wouldn't become suspicious of them.

"I wasn't expecting the snow." Bruce nodded beyond them to the icy white precipitation covering the ground. "I guess I should have watched the weather."

"I think this snowstorm caught us all by surprise." Hayes kept his voice conversational and cool. "How are the roads?"

"Icy and slick. But I came here to fish. I'm not going to let this weather stop me. I found the most magical fishing spot near this small island in the lake. Now, don't you two tell anyone about it, you hear?"

Addie couldn't just stand here like a lump talking about weather. What would be next? Sports?

This could be her opportunity to find out information.

She drew in a deep breath before starting. "Say . . . I think I met your wife. Brianna, right? I'm staying at the cabin next door, and I recognize your truck."

Addie watched Bruce's expression carefully, looking for any signs of guilt.

She saw none.

But how was that possible?

"That's right," Bruce finally said with a wide grin. "Brianna is my girl. She didn't tell me she met anyone since we've been here."

"Well, we didn't talk *that* much." Addie shrugged. "I actually stopped by last night to share some cookies with her, but no one was home. She didn't go back to Oregon early, did she? She was going to give me a recipe for some apple cinnamon bread."

That was the truth. Brianna had been baking a loaf when the two of them had talked. The treat had smelled delicious, and Brianna promised to get a copy of the recipe for Addie.

A flicker of curiosity passed Bruce's gaze before quickly disappearing. "She ran into a friend from college while she was in town, and the two of them decided to stay together for a couple of days. Then she'll come back so we can enjoy some time together. I plan on doing some fishing in the meantime."

"A friend from college?" Addie couldn't help but think what a huge coincidence that was, but she tried not to show her skepticism. "That's great that it worked out for them both to be in this area at the same time."

"The timing couldn't be better," Bruce said. "Me and the wifey could use a break from each other. We always like to say that we fight hard and love hard. But right now we're getting on each other's nerves. We're supposed to stay here two weeks. But two weeks in that cabin together is maybe two weeks too long."

Addie glanced to his backseat. The same green coat she'd seen Brianna wearing yesterday lay on the seat there.

Why would Brianna have met with her friend without her coat?

Alarm continued to race through Addie.

She stared at Bruce another moment, unsure if she could believe anything he'd just said.

What if he'd done something to Brianna?

HAYES WATCHED as Bruce's truck disappeared down the road before he turned to Addie. Her stormy expression made it clear she didn't like—or trust—the man.

He couldn't blame her. Something about this entire situation was off. But he wasn't sure the man had done anything criminal. However, the fact he'd arrived after Addie was already here did send up some red flags.

"He doesn't act like a guilty man, does he?" Hayes asked Addie.

"Did you see the coat in the backseat? It's Brianna's. Why would she be in this area without her coat? It's freezing outside."

He shrugged. "Maybe she has more than one."

Addie opened her mouth to object then shut it

again. A moment later, she said, "I keep thinking about the blood that you found on the counter at their cabin."

"Again . . . it could be because someone cut their finger. It wasn't enough blood to raise any alarms."

"Or it could be there because Bruce did something terrible to his wife."

Hayes shifted, the snow crunching beneath his feet. "As soon as I'm able to get service, I'll see what I can find out. If something truly did happen to Brianna, I don't want to look the other way. But we have to be careful about jumping to conclusions as well."

A small frown tugged at Addie's lips.

"I'm not doubting your instincts." Hayes turned to fully face her, needing to drive home the truth. "But if we go around throwing out accusations to either the police or Bruce himself, then we could actually slow down any potential investigations. We need more solid proof first."

Addie glanced up at him, still looking uncertain.

He didn't want to discourage her. In fact, his goal had always been to build her up. To help her feel more confident and not to second-guess herself. Her first marriage had destroyed her self-esteem. She'd made a lot of strides in the right direction, though. She'd begun to bloom.

Until the home invasion.

Right now, her safety was his first priority.

"I think you're doing the right thing," he continued. "I know how much you care about people. That's always been one of the things I love about you. It always will be."

Maybe Hayes shouldn't have said that. Maybe it was too much.

But he didn't take the words back. He meant them.

Addie seemed to realize that because her cheeks flushed. With her gloved hand, she pushed a stray lock of hair from her face before looking away.

Hayes pulled out his phone and held it up.

Still no signal.

He fought a frown. It was incredibly cold. The icy snow was slippery. And someone dangerous was possibly hunting them.

The only thing he liked about this situation was the fact he was with Addie.

"Let's keep walking." He nodded toward the road climbing in front of them. "I'm hoping that, once we get to the top of this ridge, maybe we can get a signal."

Addie nodded, not saying anything. Hayes couldn't read her thoughts. But he knew the whole situation had upset her.

As she took another step, her foot slipped.

She started to fall.

He reached down and caught her.

Pulled her back to her feet.

And into his arms.

Accidentally, of course.

Their faces were mere inches apart as they stared at each other.

Memories of their first kiss flashed back to him. Images of ice skating together. Neither had been naturals in the rink. The two had clung to each other as they tried to stay on their feet. They'd laughed the whole time.

Until the laughter stopped, and their gazes had locked.

Then they'd kissed—and it had been incredible.

It had continued to be incredible in the years they were married.

Hayes wished more than anything that things were different between them.

Before either of them could speak, a stick cracked in the distance and pulled him from his thoughts.

He stiffened, pushing Addie behind him.

Then he grabbed his gun and turned toward the sound, anticipating trouble.

———

Addie's heart pounded into her chest.

What if that sound had come from The Guardian? Or was it the person who'd hit Hayes on the head last night? Were they one and the same?

She didn't know.

But what if someone was watching them now?

Hayes's muscles tensed beneath her fingers.

Another stick cracked.

She held her breath as she realized the two of them were totally exposed here.

In one easy motion, Hayes pushed her farther behind him.

That was the way he was. He didn't think twice about his own safety—not when Addie was around. There weren't many people she could say that about.

Was there anyone besides Hayes who truly cared about her and her well-being?

She didn't think so.

A moment later, a moose with giant antlers moseyed from the forest.

Addie released her breath.

But her relief was only momentary.

She'd just read a brochure talking about how dangerous the animals were.

They weren't docile like deer.

No, moose could—and did—attack.

"Don't make any sudden moves." Hayes

remained tense, his gaze still on the moose. "Just let him go on his merry way."

They watched as the creature lumbered across the road, hardly giving them a second glance.

Finally, the animal reached the other side of the road and crossed into the woods as if he didn't have a care in the world.

When the moose was a good distance away, Addie and Hayes finally dared to move.

"That was . . . interesting." Hayes shoved his gun back into his holster and let out a breath.

Addie's gaze followed the creature as it crept farther and farther into the forest. "Yes, it was."

They walked silently until they reached the top of the road.

As Hayes held up his phone, hope filled his gaze. "I have a signal. Now I need to find a tow truck driver who can come help us."

Addie wished that she felt relief.

But instead, she realized this was far from being over. She'd come here after the threats being sent to her had escalated. Someone had come into her house when she wasn't home. She'd been followed home from work. She'd gotten a voicemail at the gym from someone who'd only breathed heavily on the line.

At first, she thought she'd been randomly targeted.

But then she wondered if someone Hayes had made angry was behind it. Or maybe that guy at the gym who'd shown a little too much interest. When she'd told him he wasn't welcome to come back, he'd seemed to comply. But . . .

Then Reggie's face filled her mind. Could her ex-husband somehow be haunting her from the grave?

The thought was crazy.

But he'd loved tormenting her.

Whoever The Guardian was, she feared he'd found her here.

As her phone also got a signal, a string of beeps sounded in her pocket.

She pulled out her cell and saw several text messages had come through.

Each one added to her mounting terror.

Where are you?

I'll find you.

Are you with him?

And the last one was a repeat of last night's:

He's going to die.

AFTER SEVERAL CALLS, Hayes finally found an available tow truck driver. But it would be at least three hours until he could get to them.

By Hayes's calculations, he and Addie were at least five miles from the nearest store. It wasn't as if they could walk there—not easily or quickly.

Their only real choice was to go back to the cabin and wait.

But at least this was progress.

Still, more than anything, he wanted to get Addie out of here and to safety.

Hopefully, soon enough that would happen.

As he glanced at Addie, he saw her face had gone pale. Alarm instantly rushed through him.

He stepped closer. "What happened?"

She shoved her phone back into her pocket.

"N—noth . . . nothing." Her voice trembled.

He didn't say anything, only looked at her and waited.

"I got more messages," she finally admitted, almost looking embarrassed.

"Can I see them?"

After a moment of hesitation, she pulled out her phone and showed him.

His stomach churned as he read each of them.

"How long have you been getting messages like this?" He studied her face as he waited for her answer.

She shrugged, still incredibly pale. "A few months."

A few months? That would put it at around the time Addie had asked him to leave.

Was that a coincidence?

He had a hard time thinking it was.

"Why didn't you tell me?" he asked.

She shrugged again. "I . . . don't know."

"Is that why you came here?"

She sighed and pushed a hair out of her eyes. "I was hoping to get away for a while, that maybe this would pass."

"Did you tell the police, at least?"

"No. I figured there was nothing they could do."

Hayes ran a hand over his face. "Addie . . ."

"Please don't lecture me." Her voice wavered.

"I'm not. It's just that . . . this is serious."

"It's clear this person isn't here right now. That he's looking for me."

Suddenly, Hayes's spine stiffened. He glanced around.

They shouldn't be out here. They were too exposed.

He put his hand on her lower back. "Let's get to the cabin. We can talk more later."

As they started to walk, he scanned the woods again. He didn't like the feeling creeping up his spine.

He'd been in law enforcement long enough to realize when something was off. When danger was close.

That's what he felt right now.

He didn't see anyone.

But he needed to remain on guard.

Too many places where someone could hide surrounded them.

Who would have sent Addie those texts?

Could it be someone connected with Hayes's time with Homeland Security?

Possibly.

He'd blame it on Reggie—except the man was dead.

Hayes had never met Reggie. He'd only heard about him.

But he had done some research, and he'd seen that Reggie came from a long line of troublemakers. He had a brother in prison for assault and battery. His dad had been a fugitive at one time. His mother had died in a drunk-driving accident.

Hayes hated the fact that Addie had suffered at the man's hands.

But he couldn't change the past. He could only be there for her in the present to help pick up the pieces.

———

"I know I've already said this but thank you again for driving all the way out here," Addie's voice pulled Hayes from his thoughts a few minutes later. "I didn't mean to turn your plans upside down. I had no idea this would be so complicated."

"It's okay." Hayes wanted to tell Addie that he would drop whatever he was doing at any time if she needed him.

But he'd already told her that. Addie had to come to that conclusion herself and truly believe it. Because time and time again, Hayes had tried to not only say the words, but to prove the sentiment to her.

What more could he do?

Heaviness pressed on him at the thought.

Addie tugged at her hat as the wind blew across them, sending with it another smattering of snow.

The walk back down was faster, even though they had to watch their steps. Some of the snow was finally melting, making the trek a little easier.

As they rounded a curve, the cabin came into view.

But as Hayes got closer, he realized that something wasn't right.

He grabbed Addie's arm and pulled her to a stop.

That's when he saw the words spray-painted on the front door.


**You won't get away with this.**

ADDIE'S LUNGS tightened so quickly that she could hardly breathe. She kept trying to take a deep breath, but she couldn't.

Especially as she stared at those words painted in red.

Who had done this? What did those words mean?

Beside her, Hayes glanced around, clearly searching for trouble.

She looked too but didn't see anyone.

"Hayes?" Addie's voice came out sounding almost fragile.

He continued to survey the area, completely on guard now. "How long were we gone?"

She glanced at her watch. "About two hours."

During those two hours, they hadn't seen anyone else come down this road except Bruce.

Hayes reached for his gun as he stepped closer. Addie remained behind him.

As she looked at the snowy ground, she saw the tracks from Bruce's truck. They led to his cabin, not hers.

"Someone's been here, but they tried to cover up their presence." Hayes nodded to an area of snow that had been disturbed.

He was right, Addie realized. There had been shoeprints there, but someone had brushed them away, trying to conceal them.

"What are we going to do?" Her heart beat harder as she looked up at Hayes.

Hayes rubbed his jaw. "The only person I can think of who might have seen anything is . . . Bruce."

Her throat constricted even more. "Is it even safe to talk to him?"

"I don't think we have any other choice at this point."

Addie drew in a deep breath.

She didn't like the sound of that.

---

Hayes stared at the cabin beside Addie's.

Bruce's truck was parked there, but he didn't see

the guy. Hayes could only assume the man was inside.

Addie remained slightly behind him as he started toward the neighboring cabin.

Just as they reached the gravel drive, Bruce stepped out the front door, a hunting knife in his hands.

The man's eyes widened with surprise when he spotted them. "Looks like the two of you are back from your walk. How was it?"

Hayes ignored the man's question, his gaze on Bruce's knife. He bristled, preparing himself to act if necessary.

He kept his voice calm as he asked, "Did you happen to see anyone near our cabin when you got back?"

"Addie's place?" Bruce shrugged before shaking his head. "I can't say I did. Then again, I've been inside sorting through bait and tackle. Everything okay?"

Hayes glanced at the cabin. "Someone left a message for us while we were gone. It's not exactly the welcome we'd like here in the area."

Bruce followed his gaze, and his eyes widened as if he was seeing the words for the first time. "Man . . . I've been coming to this place for a long time. Never heard of anything like that happening. It's usually so peaceful out here."

"So you haven't seen anyone hanging around?" Hayes clarified, his gaze traveling to the man's knife again.

"No, I'm sorry. I haven't heard anyone either. Then again, these lug holes don't hear like they used to." He tapped his ears, showing a small hearing aid there. "Noise-induced hearing loss. That's what my doctor said. I used to work shows for bands up and down the West Coast, and it killed my eardrums."

The man wasn't exactly acting cagey.

He *could* be telling the truth.

But as Hayes glanced through the front door, he saw a coil of rope there . . . and some black plastic bags.

HAYES'S HEART POUNDED HARDER.

The rope and plastic bags could be a coincidence. They could simply be household objects.

Or they could be something more.

Add those things with the duct tape and drops of blood . . .

But Hayes had no way of proving anything right now. All he had were unfounded suspicions.

His Homeland Security team had made a grave mistake once, based on circumstantial evidence. They'd suspected someone was a terrorist, but they'd had no proof. They'd gotten desperate and rushed the process. As a result, the whole case had ended up being thrown out.

Two days later, fifteen people had been shot and

killed in a targeted attack led by the man he should have been able to arrest.

He still blamed himself for that to this day.

"Thank you for your help," Hayes finally told Bruce. "If you do happen to see anyone around here, please let me know."

"Will do." Bruce gripped the knife with one hand and offered a salute with the other before heading back inside.

Hayes kept a hand on Addie's arm as they headed back to her place.

It wasn't until they were several feet away that he spoke. "Let me check out the inside of the cabin first. I don't think anyone got in. But I need to be certain."

Addie nodded, but Hayes could tell the situation was getting to her. Her eyes looked dull and disillusioned. He didn't like seeing her like that.

As they continued back to the cabin, he prayed that trouble would hold off for a couple more hours. That's when the tow truck would be here.

Then, with any luck, they could leave this place and not look back.

---

Addie waited outside while Hayes checked out her cabin.

The person who'd done this could still be close.

If Reggie was still alive, she'd blame him.

Thankfully, she'd left him.

She'd moved to a new place. Started a new life for herself.

But she'd lived in fear that Reggie would find her. If he did, he'd kill her. She had no doubt about that.

She continued living in fear . . . until two years after she left him when she heard he'd died of a drug overdose.

That news made her feel like she'd been set free.

Eventually, she'd met Hayes, and everything had felt so blissfully wonderful.

Until that home invasion had changed everything. Had made her realize that trouble was a close companion—one she couldn't get rid of, no matter how hard she tried.

Every once in a while, she wondered . . . what if Reggie really hadn't died? What if he'd somehow faked his death?

Could he be the one taunting her?

As her lungs tightened, she realized she needed to get a grip before anxiety claimed her.

She stepped around the cabin, toward the backside that faced Lake Tahoe.

It was so peaceful here. At least it *should* be.

Addie pulled her coat closer as she stared at the

water and the mountains majestically rising in the distance.

She'd known coming here wouldn't fix anything. But she'd needed to get away. The man who'd been tormenting her was becoming more desperate, more unhinged. She hadn't been able to handle it any longer.

However, there was no escaping who she was, and nothing would ever change that.

A moment later, the back door opened, and Hayes stepped out.

He joined her at the railing overlooking the lake. "It's clear inside."

Addie nodded but didn't say anything.

A moment of silence passed again until Hayes turned to her.

Addie sensed he wanted to say something important. She felt the tension in the air. Knew he still cared about her.

She still cared about him too, even as she tried to squash her feelings.

The task felt impossible.

But what other choice did she have?

"I haven't stopped fighting for you, you know," he murmured.

Addie's heart pounded harder.

Part of her had longed to hear those words. The

other part knew she couldn't let Hayes hold on like this.

"I didn't ask you to keep fighting for me." Her words came out just above a whisper.

"That's not something that you have to ask." Conviction edged his words.

She swallowed the lump in her throat. "I didn't ask you here so we could rekindle anything."

Nausea swirled in her gut as her words hung in the air.

Especially when she saw the hurt in his eyes.

If only she could make him understand.

But she couldn't. Not now. Not ever.

She licked her lips, her nurturing side wanting to comfort him. To take back her words. To explain everything.

But if she did that, Hayes would only become more of a target.

How could she live with herself if Hayes died because of her?

She couldn't.

The best thing she could do—the most loving thing—was to let him move on. To start again. To have a chance of happiness.

Before she could beat herself up anymore, a tow truck rumbled down the road and turned into the driveway.

"That was faster than I expected," Addie muttered.

She glanced at Hayes and saw the questions lingering in his gaze.

Then again, maybe the timing was perfect.

# CHAPTER FOURTEEN

HAYES AND ADDIE both rode in the front seat of the tow truck—Hayes in the middle. The scent of grease filled the inside of the cab, and the tow truck driver—a man in his twenties named Willie—hadn't stopped talking since he'd picked them up.

Hayes hoped to see if he could find a rental car in town. Then he would ask the driver to go back and get Addie's car also.

"Glad you found a signal," Willie muttered.

"Is that a rarity around here?" Hayes glanced at him.

"Comes with the territory." He shrugged before chomping on his chewing gum.

"That's not good when you're out in the middle of nowhere without transportation." Hayes shook his head and let out a throaty chuckle.

"You can say that again. Anyway, I'm glad you were able to call me."

They made small talk for a few more minutes.

Then Willie began to go on and on about a recent string of vandalisms in the area. Most were petty crimes—break-ins, stolen catalytic converters, a few instances of peeping toms.

More items to add to their list of things to worry about, Hayes mused with a frown.

Who would have thought things like that happened out here in such an idyllic area?

Yet, at the same time, Hayes wasn't surprised. He'd seen the worst sides of human nature in his job as a Homeland Security agent as well as while working for Vanishing Ranch.

His mind wouldn't stop going back to his conversation with Addie.

*I didn't ask you here so we could rekindle anything.*

He didn't understand her reasons for shutting him out. He'd never stopped loving her, and he never would.

Maybe he should tell her that again.

Maybe this time it would change something.

But maybe the smartest thing would be for him to just move on. However, he knew he wouldn't.

He wasn't the type to give up—especially when it was something he believed in.

And he definitely believed in his marriage, even if what Addie had done to him was the most heart-breaking experience that had ever happened in his life.

————

By the time Addie and Hayes got into town, she didn't feel better. Especially not after what the tow truck driver had said about the rash of vandalisms in the area.

The driver had dropped them off at a car rental place on Main Street before towing Hayes's rented SUV another three blocks to his shop. The man had told them it would be at least two days until he could get the tires delivered. He would order some for her car also. He'd taken that information when he picked them up.

That was when Hayes had said he needed to rent another car.

A woman sat behind a desk inside the rental agency—a woman Hayes hoped could help them.

"Good afternoon," Hayes started. "We're having some car problems and need a vehicle while we're in town. We'll take anything you've got available."

The forty-something woman glanced over the top of her glasses as she turned away from her computer.

"I'm sorry. But we actually don't have any available cars right now."

Addie felt her lungs deflate. "What?"

Hayes stepped closer. "How soon can you get something?"

"I just checked for someone else. We don't have any vehicles due back here until tomorrow evening. Unfortunately, there's been a shortage of rental cars in this area. It's been a problem for the past year or so."

Hayes pressed his eyes closed a moment.

When he opened his eyes again, he said, "So if we want to get out of town, we can't? We're stuck here?"

"I'm sorry. I've called several agencies around the area, and we're all in the same boat right now. I know this isn't what you want to hear. But if anything pops up earlier, you can leave me your name and number, and I'll get back with you as soon as I can."

"I'd appreciate that. Thanks for your time, ma'am." Hayes jotted down his information, slipped it across the desk to her, and then headed outside.

When he and Addie were back on Main Street, she turned toward him. "What are we going to do?"

Hayes released a long breath that came out in a puff of icy fog in front of him. "It doesn't sound like there's much we can do. Everyone we know lives too far away to simply drive out and pick us up."

"There has to be something we can do . . ."

"For now, we should talk to the police. I'm not sure if we can in good conscience report your neighbor for fighting with his wife. But we can tell the authorities about our tires being slashed as well as the message left on the door."

Addie nodded quickly, anxiously. "That only seems smart."

Hayes pointed down the street to the sign saying, "Sheriff's Office."

As they started walking that way, Addie's phone buzzed.

It was another text.

From the same number.

And the message was simple.

You're going to regret doing this.

# CHAPTER
# FIFTEEN

HAYES SAW the alarm on Addie's face as she stood on the sidewalk staring at her phone. "What is it?"

She started to shove her phone back in her pocket when he touched her arm.

"Addie . . . I know you want to close me out. But if you know something that can help us, then you need to share it. Our lives could depend on it. This isn't just about our broken relationship anymore."

She frowned before showing him her screen. "I got another text."

You're going to regret doing this.

Hayes sucked in a breath as he read the words.
Why would someone send that message to her?

He checked the area code. The sender was from Missouri.

Missouri?

What sense did that make? Addie wasn't from Missouri. As far as Hayes knew, she didn't have any contacts within the state.

Unless Addie knew something Hayes didn't—and that was a real possibility.

He stared at Addie, searching her gaze for the truth. "What exactly are you going to regret? Looking into what happened to your neighbor? Being here with me? Or is there something else I should know about?"

"I really don't know." She shrugged—almost too quickly.

Hayes stared at her another moment before forcing his shoulders to soften. Getting upset wouldn't help their situation. It would only set Addie back.

Before he could say anything else, she suddenly straightened. She nodded toward the coffeehouse behind them. "Listen, could you grab me an Americano? I need to run to the bathroom."

"Sure . . ."

Then she disappeared inside the coffeehouse as if in a hurry.

Addie just needed a breather before another panic attack set in.

She slipped into the bathroom and into a stall, where she closed and latched the door. She sat on the back of the toilet and pulled her feet onto the seat, desperate to disappear for a moment.

Her head throbbed.

How long could she be around Hayes without spilling everything?

*If you stay with him, he'll die.*

That was the underlying message The Guardian had told her.

But she couldn't tell Hayes that. This guy had been watching her. He would know.

She pressed her eyes closed.

As she heard the door open, she stiffened and held her breath.

But she heard nothing else.

Had someone come inside?

If so, why didn't she hear them now?

Her throat tightened as she waited.

She still heard nothing.

No movement.

Had the person left?

Leaning over, she tried to see beneath the stall door.

Finally, she saw shoes.

Her heart rate quickened when she realized those weren't women's shoes.

No, they were muddy work boots . . . belonging to a man.

Who exactly was inside this restroom with her?

Should she scream to alert Hayes? Or would that possibly be the worst mistake she could make?

# CHAPTER
# SIXTEEN

ADDIE'S HEART continued to thrum in her ears.

Was this the person who'd been sending those threats?

Had he followed her into the bathroom?

What if he'd been watching? If he'd seen her with Hayes?

And what if he'd come here now to keep true to his promise?

A lot of those texts she'd gotten today had been sent last night.

The Guardian very well could have figured out where she'd gone by now. He could be in this room with her, waiting to punish her for disobeying his orders.

Panic tried to grip her.

She couldn't let it.

Instead, she remained perfectly still.

One wrong move would give away her presence.

She couldn't chance that.

She pressed her eyes closed. *Lord, I know You must be disappointed with me . . . but please. Help!*

The man took another step.

He was coming closer.

If he tried to open this door, he would find her.

Then what would he do?

Put that knife to her throat again?

*Please, Lord . . .*

Desperation raced through her blood.

He paused in front of her door.

She could hear him breathing—a heavy, almost winded sound.

His shadow stretched across the floor.

One move, and he'd find her.

Addie's lungs tightened until she could hardly breathe.

He was toying with her, wasn't he?

A cold sweat spread across her brow.

Then the bathroom door opened again, and a woman gasped. "What do you think you're doing in here?"

Just as quickly as the man had appeared, he scrambled from the restroom.

Addie released her breath.

That could've gone so differently.

What if someone else hadn't come in?

What if he decided to come back?

She didn't know.

But she couldn't stay here and wait to find out either.

———

Hayes ordered some black coffee for himself and the Americano for Addie and then waited as the barista fixed it.

As he did, he called one of his former Homeland Security colleagues and asked him to look into his past cases to see if any of his enemies might be threatening Addie now.

His colleague, John, promised to do that and get back in touch with him.

He grabbed their drinks and then glanced down the hallway where Addie had disappeared. She'd been gone a while.

What was taking her so long?

He started to check on her just as she reappeared.

But she looked paler than before.

Instantly, his muscles stiffened. "Are you okay?"

She glanced around nervously before stepping closer.

"Want to tell me what's going on?" Hayes asked as he studied her.

"It's . . . just that someone was in the bathroom with me."

"What do you mean?"

Her chin trembled. "A man came in. I couldn't see his face. But he stood in front of the door to my stall. But then someone else walked in, and he ran."

Hayes stiffened. "Where did he go?"

"I'm not sure. I think the back door to the kitchen was open. Maybe he ran out."

He put the drinks in her hands and muttered, "Stay here!"

Then he ran toward the back of the building, determined to find answers.

# CHAPTER
# SEVENTEEN

ADDIE WAITED with dread in the coffeehouse.

She backed against the wall so she could keep an eye on everyone around her.

But no one seemed to be paying attention.

Everyone got their warm drinks and left.

She took a sip of her Americano and tried to calm her racing heart.

It did no good.

Was there anywhere she could go where trouble wouldn't find her?

It didn't seem like it.

She wanted to believe there was a light at the end of this tunnel. But was there? She didn't see how any of this would have a happy ending.

With a frown, she glanced down the hall where Hayes had disappeared.

Was he okay?

Had he caught this guy?

Her heart pounded harder with each question.

She felt another panic attack coming on and took a deep breath.

Three things she could see: her coffee, a display of pastries, a rustic table. Three things she could smell: coffee, cinnamon, and vanilla. Three things she could feel: the smooth paper cup in her hands, the thick coat around her, the plastered wall behind her.

*You're going to regret doing this.*

The words echoed in her mind.

Had that ominous text been a prelude to this moment?

She didn't know.

But if Hayes wasn't back in two minutes, she would go look for him.

———

Hayes ran out the back door and paused.

He glanced around the small parking lot behind the string of shops.

No one was there.

But that didn't mean the man was gone.

He stuffed his gun into his pocket, ready to use it

if necessary. Then he slowly walked the perimeter of the lot.

If this man had just been in the bathroom, then he couldn't be too far away.

But Hayes walked the entire perimeter, and no one was there.

Hayes supposed the man could have circled the building to the street where he had a car waiting.

With a sigh, Hayes went back into the restaurant. He ran into a server there—a woman—and asked her if she'd seen a man back here.

"I did. In the women's restroom at that."

His heart rate quickened. "Could you describe him?"

She frowned and shifted a tub of mugs from one hip to the other. "I wish I could. He had a bushy beard and a cap that was pulled down low. That was about all I noticed. He seemed embarrassed because when he saw me, he left quickly."

Hayes thanked her and then hurried back out to Addie.

As he gave her the update, her expression changed with each new fact. Disappointment that Hayes hadn't found him. Thankful that the waitress had seen him. Anxious over what would happen next.

Hayes could tell Addie was trying to hold it together but struggling.

"Let's go talk to the police," he finally said.

With coffee in hand, they walked down the road to the sheriff's office.

A few minutes later, Sheriff Steve Liberman greeted them. The fifty-something man was tall and thin with stark white hair that contrasted with his olive complexion.

He pointed to two wooden chairs on the other side of his desk. "Have a seat. How can I help you?"

They both sat across from him, and Hayes introduced himself and Addie, adding that he'd been a Homeland Security agent, and then he shared what happened to their tires as well as the message left on the cabin door and the bathroom incident.

Sheriff Liberman took notes and promised to get someone out there to investigate.

"And there's also an issue with my neighbors," Addie blurted.

Hayes fought a frown. He wasn't going to bring them up, but if Addie felt convicted that she should, then so be it.

He just didn't want to sound any alarms without the proper evidence.

He'd learned that lesson firsthand during the fiasco with Homeland Security.

# CHAPTER
# EIGHTEEN

HAYES WAITED to see how Liberman would respond.

"What about your neighbors?" The sheriff stared at Addie as he waited for her to continue.

Addie rubbed her palms on her jeans. "I talked to his wife yesterday afternoon, and she seemed shaken. She had a few bruises. Then after her husband came home that evening, I heard them arguing—really arguing. It was heated, to say the least. This morning, she's gone. Her husband claims she's staying with a friend."

Liberman narrowed his eyes. "Why would you think otherwise?"

Addie drew in a deep breath, and Hayes hoped she didn't share the fact he'd trespassed in their cabin and had seen blood. That would make this situation entirely more complicated.

"They were fighting a lot, and Brianna just seemed frightened," Addie said. "Then Bruce told us she just happened to run into a friend in the area and that she'd be gone for a couple of days. It doesn't seem like a likely story to me."

The sheriff grunted before nodding. "I do believe he's the guy who got a little rowdy down at our local watering hole last night. I'll see what I can find out. See if a woman was with him there. We can do a quick welfare check while we're out there. We can be subtle."

Addie's shoulders softened. "Thank you. It would make me feel a lot better."

"I have one of my deputies at another scene right now, but as soon as he's done I'll send him out. Sound good?"

Addie nodded. "That sounds great."

"And if you need a ride back, we can help you out with that too. But it will be a couple of hours."

"We'd really appreciate that," Hayes said. "If you could give us a call, we'll be hanging out around town until then."

"Will do."

They left their information with him before heading outside.

As they did, Addie's phone rang. "It's my exercise studio."

She put it to her ear and paced away. A moment later, she returned. Her face looked pale again.

Hayes braced himself for more bad news. "Did something else happen?"

"The studio was broken into last night . . . they didn't discover it until they got in to work this morning. The place was ransacked. The mirrors smashed. Someone even took a box cutter to the specialty flooring."

His breath caught. "What? That sounds vindictive. Not your typical break-in. Did they call the police?"

Addie nodded as moisture filled her gaze. "They did. But. . ."

"What is it?"

"Danielle is missing. No one has seen her since last night." Her face crumbled. "Oh, Hayes . . . do you think this guy did something to her?"

———

Addie's thoughts were spinning.

She couldn't believe Danielle was missing.

What if this was all because Addie had come here? A cry stuck in her throat.

"I've got to go find her," she finally muttered.

Hayes grabbed her arm. "That's not going to help. It's just going to put you right back where this guy wants you."

"But . . . I just can't stay here and not do anything."

"Let me make a few calls."

She went still. "What kind of calls?"

"I can see if some of my friends can check this out. It's the better option. First, because they're professionals. Second, because you won't be safe if you go back there now."

"But Danielle . . ." A tear ran down her cheek as she imagined what her friend might be going through.

"Did your friends report her disappearance to the police?"

Addie nodded.

"Then they'll be looking into whatever happened with her, okay? My guys are going to help."

She nodded again.

"I'm going to make those calls now, okay?" Hayes locked gazes with her. "While I do, you should call your insurance company. I know it seems unimportant considering that Danielle is missing, but you don't want too much time to pass."

As anxiety tried to overtake her, Addie pulled her phone from her pocket.

When would this nightmare end?

# CHAPTER
# NINETEEN

FIFTEEN MINUTES LATER, Addie and Hayes found a small restaurant called Regina's, which featured both American and Italian food. Neither had eaten since breakfast, and they needed to pass some time anyway until one of the sheriff's deputies could take them back to their cabin.

The inside of the restaurant was simple with red and white checkered curtains and tablecloths and an old linoleum floor. But the place was warm, and the scent of garlic and bread seemed welcoming.

Hayes had ordered a chicken parmesan sandwich, and Addie had gotten a salad with fruit and chicken.

Their food was delivered quickly, for which she was grateful. She was hungrier than she thought. Plus, being here with Hayes brought back so many memories of the small-town restaurants they'd once loved exploring. They'd always tried different dishes and shared them. The more hole-in-the-wall the place was, the better.

Hayes had already called some of his friends. They'd promised to look into Danielle.

But Addie couldn't stop thinking about her friend. She was the most loving, giving, and generous person Addie knew.

She didn't deserve to be pulled into this.

"I feel like we have two separate issues going on here," Hayes started after they prayed. "You have this guy who is threatening you and who may have grabbed Danielle. Then we have Brianna and Bruce."

"You don't think they're connected?"

"I don't think so. You did say Bruce and Brianna arrived after you, correct?"

She nodded.

"I suppose there's a chance they could have followed you here. But I don't believe that's likely. Still, we should keep the idea in the back of our minds."

"That's probably wise."

A moment of silence passed before Addie asked, "You really think your friends might find something out?"

"I do. They're good at what they do. For now, let's just try to wait it out. I know it's hard."

She nodded.

A moment later, Hayes shifted again. "I've been thinking about ways to follow up on Brianna."

Her eyebrows shot up. Addie figured Hayes would simply dismiss her concerns now that they'd informed the sheriff about what happened. Not that Hayes was a dismissive kind of guy. He wasn't.

But, thanks to Reggie, Addie's brain was programmed to anticipate her opinions being trivialized.

People just didn't seem to take her seriously.

Didn't seem to care.

At least, they hadn't until Hayes had come into her life.

He was one of a kind.

More regret wafted inside her.

———

"Did you come up with any ideas?" Addie cut a piece of her chicken and picked through her salad for all the good pieces of lettuce.

Thinking about Brianna was a good distraction from thinking about Danielle. Hayes was right—they just had to wait right now. There was nothing more they could do. If The Guardian had grabbed her, he'd probably let Addie know. He'd probably send a text.

She cut out a thick, browning stalk on a piece of romaine and frowned.

Hayes had always seemed amused when she did that, but she couldn't help herself.

Nothing ruined a good salad faster than bad lettuce.

"If we can find out Brianna's last name, maybe we can find a picture on social media," Hayes said as he spread his napkin across his lap. "This town isn't that big. Brianna would've probably stopped at the general store for supplies or to get gas at some point. Or if she did run into her friend, the two of them could be staying at the inn. If we can find a picture of her, we can show it around and see if anyone has seen her recently."

A surge of comfort filled Addie.

Hayes wasn't dismissing her.

He wanted to help.

Relief softened her shoulders. She'd been so afraid he'd tell her she needed to move on—and that was the last thing she wanted.

She stabbed more chicken and an apple slice with her fork. "That's a great idea. But how are we going to find out her last name?"

"There's a rental company sign on her cabin. Maybe if we can contact this company, we can ask a few questions."

Brilliant. Why hadn't Addie thought of that?

But . . . she shifted and lowered her fork. "You really think they're going to give us her last name just because we ask?"

Hayes shrugged as if he wasn't worried. "Not at first. But maybe with some persuasion, we can get it out of them."

He definitely had a set of skills she didn't.

Addie glanced down at her salad, hardly hungry now. "Thank you. I know I keep saying that. But I mean it. I think Bruce did something to Brianna."

"Why are you so confident?" Hayes squinted as he studied her face.

Addie let out a long breath as she tried to collect her thoughts. "It's like this . . . I had a friend once who hated celery. If someone added just a little bit of celery to anything she was eating, she could immediately taste it because she hated celery that much. I feel like it's that same way with abusers. Now that I know what one is like, I can spot them a mile away."

Hayes stared at her another moment before nodding. "Good explanation. Let's finish up here, and then we'll see what we can find out."

Relief washed through her. He'd understood, and his support meant the world to her.

# CHAPTER
# TWENTY

HAYES'S THOUGHTS were all over the place as he finished eating his sandwich.

He wanted to support Addie.

But he also wanted to keep her safe.

He wanted to whisk her far away from here.

But he didn't want to pull her from a situation where she felt called to help.

Yet, if her life was on the line, he couldn't simply sit back and watch something bad happen to her.

So he figured it was better if he stayed close for as long as she'd let him.

He paid at the restaurant, and then they found the office for the vacation rental agency. The building was located on Main Street and within easy walking distance. Thankfully, it had warmed up some outside and walking wasn't miserably cold.

Ten minutes later, he had Brianna's last name. The woman working at the vacation rental agency had been very chatty—almost too much so. Thankfully, it had worked in their favor. They'd also found out the Newtons' rental had been last minute.

That meant they could have shown up here at Lake Tahoe because they were somehow tracking Addie. He had no proof or motive yet, but it was a possibility.

Once on the sidewalk, Hayes leaned against the building, pulled out his phone, and searched various social media sites as he looked for a picture of Brianna Newton. It didn't take long for him to find her.

He held up his phone and showed Addie a picture of a smiling woman with curly blonde hair. "This is her, right?"

Addie's eyes widened. "Yes, it is. Has she posted anything recently?"

He scrolled through Brianna's page and frowned. "It's hard to tell for sure. Her account is private, but she has a few public photos. I don't see any pictures of her with Bruce. However, there is a picture here of her with another woman. I wonder if this is the friend she met with."

Addie stared at the picture before shrugging. "Your guess is as good as mine."

He scrolled a couple more minutes before releasing a long breath.

"I could send her a friend request," Addie offered. "Maybe I can see more that way."

"I suppose it can't hurt to try."

Addie tapped a few things on her cell phone, clearly anxious for answers.

When she finished, she slid her phone back into her pocket. "Now we wait, I guess."

"We do. But in the meantime, let's go ask some questions. Maybe someone around here has seen her and knows something."

---

Forty-five minutes later, the two of them had hit all of the spots in town where Brianna might have visited —including the inn.

No one had seen her.

At the general store, their last stop, Hayes struck up a casual conversation with the clerk. Based on some stickers on the register, the man appeared to be a Raiders fan. One of Hayes's best friends from childhood played for the team.

After several minutes of chitchat, Hayes got to the heart of the matter.

He found a picture of Brianna online and showed it to the clerk. "Have you seen this woman?"

"Can't say I have."

"What about him?" Hayes found a picture of Bruce and showed the man.

"As a matter of fact, I have." The older gentleman stared at Hayes's phone. "He's been in a few times, actually."

"Always by himself?" Addie stepped closer as if she didn't want to miss a single part of this conversation.

"Yep. Always by himself."

Hayes shifted before continuing. "Could you see anyone in his truck waiting for him?"

"No truck. He was in a car."

"A car?" Hayes repeated, his brow furrowed. "You sure?"

The clerk nodded slowly but certainly. "Absolutely. The sedan looked as if it could break down at any minute. It was rust-colored with no fender and plastic was taped over one of the windows. Kind of hard to forget."

What sense did that make? Did Bruce and Brianna each have their own vehicle?

"Sounds like a memorable car. You didn't happen to see the license plate, did you? See what state it was from?"

"Sorry. Eyes aren't that good."

Hayes tapped his knuckles against the well-used counter. "Thank you for your help."

"Of course." The man nodded.

Hayes and Addie left the store knowing a little more—but not enough to find Brianna.

# CHAPTER
# TWENTY-ONE

"DID Bruce and Brianna bring two vehicles on this trip?" Addie glanced up at Hayes as they paused outside beneath a faded awning. "I've only seen a truck at the cabin."

"I'm not sure."

"What are you thinking?" Addie waited, studying Hayes's face.

Hayes let out a long breath. "Let's say Bruce *did* do something to Brianna. What would he have done with her body? Dumped her in the woods?"

"Or the lake." Addie shrugged. "That's what they sometimes do on TV."

"I looked in the back of his truck when I passed it. I didn't see any blood. Even if I did, he would've said it was from hunting."

"But if he'd wrapped her in trash bags and duct tape, maybe any blood was contained."

"That's possible." Hayes let out another long breath. "Listen, I'm going to take a breather and call my friends back at Vanishing Ranch."

"You already called them, though."

"I called them about checking on Danielle. Now I'm going to call them about coming here to act as backup."

Addie continued to study him. "Okay, but . . . they're hours away."

"I know if I ask, Jesse or Mateo will come. One of them would at least bring a car. But I also know they're really busy right now."

"I don't want to call them away from what they're doing." A frown tugged at her lips. "It's important work. I say we catch that ride back to the cabin and wait for our tires to come in."

Hayes raised his eyebrows, appearing as if he were fighting exhaustion. "We go back to a cabin that is located directly beside someone who might have just killed his wife? To the cabin where somebody has left us a message and slashed our tires?"

"You'll be with me." Addie's voice sounded soft as she said the words. "I'm always safe with you."

Her words caused a strange emotion to pass through his gaze.

But she didn't want to read too much into it.

Hayes stared at his phone another moment as if contemplating what to do.

Finally, he put the device back into his pocket.

"I'll give this until my SUV tires are replaced," he said. "After that, I won't make you leave, but I'm going to strongly encourage it."

"But if I leave . . . where would I go? San Diego doesn't seem safe."

His jaw visibly tightened. "You're right. It's not. But I'll find you somewhere that is."

———

Addie tried not to feel pleased.

But she did.

She thought for sure that Hayes would insist she leave.

But he hadn't.

That was a good thing because she didn't know if she could walk away from this situation without any answers.

Because what if in a few days she heard a news story about Brianna? If she heard that her body had been found? What if Addie had the opportunity to help and didn't do everything in her power to stop an innocent woman from being harmed or killed?

She wouldn't be able to live with herself if that was the case.

For so many years while she was married to Reggie, Addie had prayed that someone would see her struggle and step in to help.

For seven years, that hadn't happened.

Until Amy came along.

Addie had met Amy in a step aerobics class, and the two had instantly become friends. As Addie had gotten to know Amy more, Addie somehow found the courage to tell Amy about her struggles.

Amy had been the one who'd encouraged Addie to leave Reggie. Who'd said that their relationship wasn't healthy.

That Addie was in danger.

It had still taken several months. Finally, with Amy's help, Addie had left him.

But now, Amy was dead. The Guardian had killed her. The police hadn't said that, but Addie felt certain of it.

Moisture rushed to her eyes.

What if this guy killed Danielle now?

She swallowed a deep breath.

Knowing that Reggie was dead had helped Addie move on. His looming threats had died with him, and she'd begun the long, arduous journey of healing.

Hayes had helped with that. Until tragedy struck again.

The home invasion had turned her world upside down a second time.

Hayes's phone buzzed, bringing Addie from her thoughts.

He checked his messages and, a moment later, he told her a sheriff's deputy was ready to take them back to the cabin. He would pick them up in front of the general store.

A few minutes later, the deputy pulled up on the street in front of them.

But Addie knew they'd eventually have to finish this conversation.

## CHAPTER
## TWENTY-TWO

HAYES TRIED to concentrate on figuring out how everything tied together as he and Addie rode back to the cabin in the deputy's cruiser.

But he couldn't stop thinking about Danielle.

He hoped Addie's friend was okay.

His thoughts drifted back to Addie's other friend, Amy, who'd died in a house fire about a month before the home invasion. Investigators had said her death wasn't suspicious.

But what if her death was somehow connected?

He didn't dare bring that up in front of Addie. But the thought wouldn't leave his mind. He suspected she thought the same thing.

His thoughts then drifted back to his marriage.

Hayes hadn't been perfect. But he tried to own up to his mistakes. The times when he worked too much. When he should've taken more vacations. When he should have been home more—like on the night of the home invasion.

But he'd earnestly tried to be the man Addie deserved.

It still haunted him that he hadn't been. That he hadn't lived up to her expectations.

At the same time, he wasn't sure how he could have changed anything. Communication was vital, and Addie had closed herself off to him. It truly was a two-way street.

"I thought I'd give you guys an update," the sheriff's deputy said from the front seat.

His name was Ned Clark, and he appeared to be fresh from the academy with his baby face and eager disposition.

"I actually went down and talked to Bruce myself," Clark said. "I was already out this way. Anyway, seemed like a nice guy."

"What did he say?" Hayes didn't want to go down the rabbit trail of Bruce being a nice guy. Criminals seemed like nice guys all the time. It didn't mean anything.

"He told me the same story he told you," Deputy Clark said. "His wife ran into someone she knew in town. The two of them aren't staying at the inn, however. They're staying at a different cabin."

"Are you going to follow up on that?" Addie's voice cracked with tension.

Clark shrugged. "I don't think I need to. Mr. Newton had a video call with her while I was there. I saw her with my own eyes. She talked to me. Said that she was fine."

Hayes glanced at Addie, trying to read her reaction.

She frowned. He knew she wasn't upset because Brianna was okay. She was upset because her instincts had been wrong.

He wanted to reach over and squeeze her hand.

But he didn't dare.

"We appreciate you doing that," Hayes told Deputy Clark instead. "And you wrote up a report on the slashed tires and the message that was spray-painted on our door?"

"We did. We'll be looking into it. We do have some troublemakers here in this area. Their crimes aren't too serious, thankfully. But we're still trying to track down who's behind some petty vandalisms."

"Petty vandalisms?" Hayes repeated, even though he'd heard the tow truck driver talking about them.

Clark shrugged. "We think it's some locals who don't like the fact this side of the lake is becoming more and more popular. They don't want it to turn into South Lake Tahoe, you know? We're trying to pinpoint who the culprits are."

"Maybe someone who wants to scare visitors away?"

Clark slowly nodded. "Most definitely."

Hayes frowned. He had a feeling there was entirely more to the story than this.

Because hitting him over the head, slashing their tires, and painting a message on their cabin was entirely more serious than petty vandalisms meant to scare away visitors.

Something dangerous—and maybe deadly—was happening in these woods.

———

Addie felt the awkwardness between her and Hayes as the deputy dropped them off at the cabin.

Now they were stuck here. Just the two of them.

She was happy Brianna was okay, but she felt foolish that she'd been so wrong.

But *had* she been wrong? What if Bruce had paid someone to pretend to be his wife? What if that really hadn't been Brianna the deputy had spoken with?

Or was Addie overreaching here?

She wasn't sure.

There was also the possibility that Deputy Clark

was right. The troublemakers who'd been haunting this area could have left that message and slashed their tires.

But would those people really go as far as to hit Hayes over the head?

She found that hard to believe.

Maybe—just maybe—someone might go to that extreme if Hayes had stumbled upon someone in the middle of committing a crime. It wasn't as if this person had tried to kill him.

But that still didn't explain the text messages Addie was getting or the fact her studio had been vandalized and Danielle was missing. Her studio was far from here—a day's drive.

Her head swirled with all the information.

She and Hayes thanked Deputy Clark and then headed toward the cabin.

As soon as the deputy drove away, movement caught the corner of her eye.

She glanced at the cabin beside them in time to see Bruce storming toward them. His shoulders appeared tight, and his steps quick.

He was angry, she realized.

Addie braced herself for the confrontation that was about to happen.

HAYES MOVED in front of Addie as soon as he saw Bruce heading their way.

Based on the set of the man's shoulders and the way his nostrils flared, he wasn't happy.

Bruce paused a couple of feet from them, accusation in his eyes. "What do you two think you're doing reporting me to the sheriff?"

Hayes knew the best thing to do in this situation was to remain calm. "We were just concerned because we hadn't seen Brianna. No harm intended."

"I've been nothing but nice to you, and you report me to the sheriff behind my back?" Bruce shoved his finger into his own chest. "I told you Brianna was staying with a friend."

"We just wanted to be certain." Addie's voice

sounded thin with fear, but she didn't back down. "We heard the arguments and . . ."

"It was just an argument! I didn't lay a hand on my wife. And I don't appreciate that insinuation."

"We apologize again for causing trouble." Hayes didn't entirely mean the words, but fighting about it right here wouldn't help the situation.

Bruce jutted his finger out—toward them this time. "Stay away from me and stay off my property. Both of you. Do you understand?"

"We do." Hayes kept his voice even as he said the words.

Bruce turned on his heel and stomped back to his cabin.

———

Addie waited until Bruce walked away before she turned to Hayes. "What are we going to do?"

"I don't know what else there is to do." He ran a hand over his face. "Other than this vandalism, our tires, and the man who struck me last night, there's no evidence of any other crimes. Sure, the text messages are threatening. But they aren't going to prove anything."

"Could we trace the sender?"

"We could try, but I'm betting it's from a burner phone."

Her gaze traveled to the cabin beside them as Bruce slammed his door after going inside. "He's hiding something."

"He very well could be. We just need to stay vigilant. That's all I can say."

Addie studied Hayes another moment, searching for the truth in his gaze.

She'd never expected him to quit his job. To make such a drastic life change.

She'd wondered about his thoughts behind it.

"Want to take a walk?" Hayes asked.

She nodded, knowing the upcoming conversation was inevitable.

They began walking away from Bruce's cabin and toward the lake.

Her thoughts drifted to Danielle again, and she lifted another silent prayer for her friend's safety. She hoped that maybe this was all a misunderstanding—even though she knew it probably wasn't.

What if The Guardian had taken her friend?

She pressed her eyes closed for a moment before shifting her thoughts.

"Do you ever miss your connections with Homeland Security?" she asked Hayes as they walked. She needed to do something to get her mind off Danielle, and talking about Hayes's job just might do the trick. "The resources you had at your disposal?"

"If you're asking if I miss my old job . . . sometimes. Other times, I know working for Vanishing Ranch was the best move for us . . . I mean . . . me. It was best for *me*."

Addie's throat suddenly went dry.

Even with what she'd put him through, he was still thinking of her.

They paused on the rocky shore of the lake and stared out at it.

She rubbed her burning throat before asking, "Why did you quit? I thought you loved your job."

"I thought it was time for some changes. For a more flexible schedule."

Was it because of her? Had he made the change because he felt guilty over not being there during that home invasion?

Addie couldn't bring herself to ask the question. Hayes had no reason to feel guilty. But she'd never be able to convince him of that.

"Do you like the new job?" she asked instead.

"It's fulfilling to feel like I can help protect people."

His words hung in the air.

Addie heard the guilt. Heard the pain.

And she wanted to correct him.

Why did the situation have to be so complicated?

She cleared her throat, trying to get her thoughts and emotions under control. "As soon as your tires are fixed or we get a rental car, you're out of here, aren't you?"

His gaze caught hers. "Not without you. You could come to Vanishing Ranch with me. I could keep you safe there. If Brianna wanted to come, she could too."

Against her wishes, her heart fluttered.

Why did she still have this reaction to him?

"I never intended to put you in the middle of this situation when I called you for advice," she started, needing to make herself clear.

"I know you don't want anything to do with me. But as far as I'm concerned, we're a team. I can't let you go into this alone, especially since we don't know who is behind the things that are going on."

"Hayes . . ." Addie's voice cracked.

She wanted to tell him he should lose all hope. But she couldn't do that. However, the longer she was around him, the more likely it was that the truth would eventually come out.

What would happen then?

The scar on her back began to ache as it always did when she remembered the pain she'd endured at The Guardian's hands.

"What do you think we should do now?" She glanced at the sun as it quickly sank in the distance, scattering darkness around them.

He placed his hand on the small of her back, sending another round of flutters and tingles up her spine. "It's been a long day. Let's go inside."

However, being in a cabin alone with Hayes seemed like a terrible idea with her feelings exploding as they were.

HAYES WATCHED as Addie pulled out some ingredients to make cookies. It was what she always did when she was stressed and unable to settle down.

Then she gave the treats away, unwilling to eat them herself. She would recite how much exercise she would have to do to burn off the calories from eating just one.

His mind raced as he tried to figure out the best plan of action. If only he could get a cell phone signal, that would make everything a lot easier.

"What if we aren't able to get a rental car?" Addie asked as she began mixing the flour and sugar. "Or if the tires really do take two days to come in? We're going to be here for a long time without transportation."

"If that's the case, we'll figure something out."

Addie stared at him a moment.

Then she began to stir the dough again.

Hayes wanted nothing more than to grab her arm. To stop the movement. To pull her into a bear hug and tell her everything would be okay.

He'd be lying if he didn't admit that he had some hard feelings. He'd do anything to get back together with her. But she'd totally broken his heart and hadn't even respected him enough to tell him why she'd insisted he leave.

He felt as if he deserved an explanation, at least. That way he could know whether or not he needed to move on. But as it stood now, he was simply stranded in a place of confusion.

She paused with the bowl in her hands and glanced out the window. "Bruce is fishing."

Hayes moved behind her, probably standing too close, and peered out also.

Sure enough, Bruce stood on the edge of the lake, his fishing line in the water—despite the descending darkness outside.

Was he a cold-blooded killer who'd offed his wife and then continued on with life as if nothing had happened?

Hayes wasn't sure.

But he didn't like the thought of it.

He glanced at Addie again, anxious to figure things out and get her to safety.

He prayed this would all be resolved soon, especially as danger continued to squeeze closer.

———

"Addie . . . why don't you sit down?" Hayes took the bowl from her hands and set it on the counter. "We can put that in the fridge in a minute."

She didn't argue as he grabbed her arm and tugged her down onto the couch beside him.

Her cheeks heated. Mostly because she wanted to reach out to him. To fall into his arms. To do more than she was allowed.

"Are you afraid of hurting me?" Hayes's gaze searched hers. "I can handle whatever you have to say. I'd rather know than just being kept in this state of uncertainty."

His words knocked the air out of her lungs.

Of course, he knew there was more to this. He was smart.

"Hayes . . ." She licked her lips.

Addie caught herself as she started to open up to him.

What if that was a terrible idea?

He reached toward her and pushed some stray hairs from her eyes.

As he touched her head, electricity jolted through her.

She wanted so badly for things to go back to the way that they used to be. Was that hoping for too much? Was she simply setting herself up for something that would never happen?

"You can trust me," he murmured reassuringly. "More than anything, I want you to know that."

She rubbed her throat as anxiety bubbled inside her.

"I've been getting threats," she finally blurted. "More than the texts I told you about."

His eyes widened. "For how long?"

She licked her lips again, uncertain how much to say. "For a while now."

*Since the home invasion.* She didn't want to tell him that, though. He'd only blame himself even more.

His gaze hardened with concern. "What kind of threats?"

"It started off with text messages like the ones you saw. But it progressed quickly. I'm pretty sure someone has been going in and out of the house as he pleases."

"In our—your—house? Again? What did he do?" Apprehension edged his voice.

She still lived in their little thousand-square-foot house. She'd had so much fun decorating it and making the space special for her and Hayes. She'd filled it with memories of her time with Hayes—pictures and knickknacks and wedding gifts.

Hayes hadn't tried to take the house from her. He'd let her have it. And her car.

But she hadn't asked for anything else. No money. No anything.

It didn't seem fair to ask for more.

Money had definitely been tight lately, to say the least.

"He didn't do anything," Addie finally said. "I think he just wanted to let me know that he was in control."

Their gazes connected, and Addie could see the emotions swirling in Hayes's eyes.

"Why didn't you tell me?" His voice sounded low and filled with hurt. "I could have helped."

Before she could answer, movement outside the window caught her eye.

She grabbed Hayes's arm and nodded. "I think that's Bruce. He's leaving the cabin."

HAYES WANTED MORE than anything to finish this conversation. He and Addie had made more progress today than they had in the past four months.

But if Bruce was moving, Hayes knew they couldn't keep talking as if nothing had happened.

Instead, he paced toward the window and peered out.

Sure enough, Bruce stepped from his cabin into the darkness. He crouched low as if he didn't want to be seen.

But he didn't head toward his truck.

He traveled toward the woods behind his place instead.

Interesting. Where could he be going at this time

of night? And why trek through the woods? Without a flashlight, at that?

The only reason the man wouldn't have a flashlight would be because he didn't want to be seen. He wanted to be sneaky.

Hayes grabbed his coat as he started toward the door. "I'm going to follow him."

Immediately, Addie was behind him. "I'm going with you. I'm safer with you than I am alone."

There were those words again.

Just as before, her statement did something to his heart. Made it pound harder and faster.

Finally, he nodded. "If we're going to follow Bruce then we need to get moving. Grab your coat."

She scrambled away from him, quickly getting ready.

But Hayes hoped he didn't regret this.

———

Addie quickly slipped her jacket on and then she and Hayes headed outside.

"We have to be quiet," Hayes whispered. "We can't let Bruce know we're following him."

She nodded and pulled her scarf higher around her neck and face.

The cold was almost biting now that it was nighttime.

When Hayes took her hand and led her into the woods, Addie didn't pull away. In fact, she felt as if she could hold onto him all day. Not that Hayes gripped her hand to be romantic. The motion was simply practical in these circumstances.

But their conversation wouldn't stop echoing in her mind.

He still cared about her. That was clear. Even after everything she'd put him through, his gaze and voice still held affection.

Was it a mistake to share with him what she had?

She still wasn't sure.

And she probably wouldn't be for a while.

They walked through the woods. Through the darkness. Away from the safety of the cabin.

Addie had meant what she said. She knew as long as she was with Hayes that she would be okay. He wasn't invincible. He wasn't Superman. But he would do everything in his power to keep her safe.

She wanted to talk to him as they walked, but she didn't dare say a word. All her concentration needed to be on watching her steps.

If she stepped on a branch or kicked a rock, it could alert Bruce that they were behind him. She couldn't chance that.

Because what if he *had* done something to Brianna? What if he was going out here now to bury her body? If that video call had just been a ruse of some sort?

Addie's throat tightened so quickly she could hardly breathe.

Why else would he be sneaking out here under the cover of night?

She and Hayes continued walking, probably thirty more minutes into the dark, almost creepy, forest.

Even though Hayes followed the man's tracks, they'd yet to lay eyes on Bruce.

Then a voice floated across the stillness.

Hayes stopped and placed a finger to his lips.

They paused behind a tree and waited.

That voice belonged to Bruce.

He spoke in low tones to someone else.

Addie's pulse quickened.

If they could overhear part of this conversation, maybe they could figure out what was going on.

# CHAPTER
# TWENTY-SIX

THE FACT that Bruce had snuck out at night to meet someone in the woods didn't look good, Hayes mused. The only reason people usually did that was if they were hiding something. He would bet that was the case now also.

He moved closer to a ponderosa pine, careful not to be seen or heard. Thankfully, the cover of trees blocked the moonlight and helped conceal him and Addie.

Did this nighttime outing have something to do with Brianna?

It seemed like a good possibility.

He only prayed he and Addie didn't find the woman injured—or worse. He wasn't sure if Addie could handle that.

Bruce was meeting with another man. He couldn't see the other guy or make out his features. Nor could he decipher the conversation. Not yet.

But the men's voices rose as they walked together.

As Bruce and his friend disappeared around the bend, Hayes quietly followed behind them with Addie.

A moment later, he heard water gently lapping against the shore.

They'd looped around the woods and then headed to the lake about a quarter mile away from the cabins, he realized.

Had that been on purpose? Was it because this area was more secluded? Because there were no neighbors out here spying on them?

Or maybe Bruce knew Hayes and Addie were following him, and he was trying to throw them off his trail. But, if that was the case, why not simply walk along the shoreline instead of taking the long way around?

Questions pounded in his head.

Something wasn't right. He wasn't sure what yet. But there was definitely something happening.

"I told you this was a bad idea," Bruce said. "We need to get rid of it."

That time his words were loud and clear.

Get rid of it? Could he be talking about a body?

Addie gripped his arm as she crouched beside him. Her breathing was shallow, and she trembled as they waited.

"Okay, I get it," the other man said. "Let's just get this over with."

The next moment, Hayes heard water splashing.

He motioned for Addie to stay where she was.

Then he crept closer for a better look.

As he got nearer to the lake, he saw that Bruce and the other man had gotten into a small rowboat.

They were now rowing toward the center of the lake.

---

"Why in the world would they go out there in the dark?" Addie asked as she stared at Bruce's retreating figure.

"I have no idea." Hayes shook his head, his gaze still on the boat as it disappeared into the darkness. "If they needed to get to the other side of the lake, why not just drive?"

This whole situation grew more perplexing all the time.

"I didn't recognize the voice of the man he was with," Addie murmured. "Did you?"

"I didn't. But I haven't met that many people around here either."

"What now?" Addie looked up at him, waiting for his next call.

Hayes frowned before shaking his head. "There's nothing else we can do here. We can't exactly get on a boat and follow them across the lake. I don't think we would want to, anyway. It seems dangerous with the cold like it is. I know the lake doesn't ever freeze solid because it's too deep. But the edges get icy."

"So we go back to the cabin?" Her voice cracked —but just slightly.

Hayes stared at her another moment before nodding. "Yes, we need to get back. It's cold out here, and it's getting late. We can reevaluate this again in the morning."

Addie would be lying if she denied the disappointment biting at her.

She wanted more.

She wanted answers.

Instead, she gripped Hayes's hand again as he began leading her back through the woods.

She was glad that he was with her.

Everything around them looked the same right now. Her sense of direction was totally shot. Hayes had always teased her about it. Had said she could get lost in a closet.

But as soon as they got back inside the cabin, she froze and pointed at something on the floor.

Wet footprints.

And they didn't belong to her or Hayes.

# CHAPTER
# TWENTY-SEVEN

"STAY HERE," Hayes muttered.

He withdrew his gun as he stepped forward.

Someone had been inside their cabin while they were gone.

He didn't like the thought of that.

Carefully, he followed the prints.

He'd guess they belonged to a man based on their size.

The tracks led to Addie's bedroom and then back out and into the kitchen.

"Hayes?" Addie's voice sounded thin with fear as she waited.

He checked the rest of the place before turning to her.

"No one's here." He stepped back toward her.

"What are you going to do now?"

"I'm going to track these prints outside and see what I can find out."

Addie remained behind him as they followed the prints down the back deck and across the ground.

They continued . . . all the way to Bruce and Brianna's cabin.

Hayes paused near the neighboring cabin.

What sense did this make? Hayes mused.

They'd seen Bruce leave. These weren't his prints.

Based on the size of them, they weren't Brianna's either.

Besides, there were no tire marks in the snow. If someone had been out here, how had they gotten here?

As he glanced at Bruce's cabin, the questions continued to pound at his temples.

He had a decision to make.

———

Addie's heart pumped in her chest as she saw Hayes studying Bruce's cabin.

What exactly was going on here?

She wasn't sure.

All she really knew was that danger zipped like electricity through the air.

One wrong step might mean the end of her. The end of Hayes.

Suddenly, she realized what a bad idea it was for her to come here to the once idyllic-looking cabin.

"Stay here," Hayes muttered.

He reached for the door.

It was unlocked.

Addie's gut clenched as he pushed it open.

Hayes stepped inside. As he did, Addie prayed fervently that he'd be safe. That this wasn't a trap.

Because if Bruce hadn't left these footprints, then someone else had. Someone who could very well still be in this cabin right now.

Images of the home invasion flooded back to her.

She'd been sitting on her couch working on a schedule for her exercise classes when she'd heard something outside. Before she could even stand, the door had burst open and a masked man had rushed inside.

He had a knife.

He'd held it out toward her and instructed that she needed to do everything he said or she'd die.

Addie had no choice but to listen.

He'd told her to sit in a chair. Then he'd tied her up.

She'd assumed he'd simply rob her—and he did

take a few things, probably to throw the police off his scent.

Instead, his real goal was to taunt her.

He talked to her about her past. About Reggie. About Amy.

About Chip.

How had he even known all of those things?

It was because the invasion was personal, she'd realized.

He'd threatened her with his knife. Had dragged it across her throat. Over her arm. Over her face.

She'd never felt so much terror.

Then he'd shown her the pictures of Hayes. On the job. With a red laser target from a gun on him.

If Addie didn't continue to do everything he said, Hayes would die. The man told her she had to follow his instructions down to the letter and not tell a soul. If she broke their agreement, he would know.

He sent her pictures and texts to prove that he had eyes and ears everywhere.

Had he left cameras and microphones in her house and car?

Maybe.

Addie had been too terrified to look for the devices. She feared if he saw her, he'd do something drastic.

That had led to her life being totally turned

upside down. He'd told her to leave Hayes. To not explain anything. To push him out of her life.

She'd debated what to do for a week after the home invasion happened. But then one night the man had been waiting for her in the backseat of her car. He'd placed the knife to her neck again. Reminded her of the stakes.

To prove his point, he'd taken his cigarette and jammed it into her back—she still had the scar there to remind her of the pain. Then he'd shown her a video on his phone—a video of Hayes being shot at. He'd said he missed on purpose.

Hayes, who'd been on assignment, and his team had assumed the shots had come from someone associated with a case they were working.

They hadn't.

The Guardian had done it. He'd made it clear that killing Hayes was within the realm of possibility.

Tears pressed at her eyes. Pushing Hayes from her life had been the hardest thing she'd ever done.

Hayes returned, snapping Addie from her thoughts as he shook his head. "No one's here."

"But the footprints . . ."

"It's weird, I know. And I can't explain them. But Bruce and Brianna's place is empty."

She rubbed her arms. "Is there anything strange inside?"

"Not that I see. I thought I saw some duct tape and black plastic bags earlier, but they're gone now."

"What would Bruce have done with them?" Her thoughts raced.

"I suppose he could've stashed them in his truck. It's really hard to say what's going on right now. But whatever it is, it's all strange and unnerving."

Addie nodded.

She could tell by Hayes's voice that he didn't like this any more than she did.

"What now?" She licked her lips.

"Now we get back to our place and hunker down for the night, and we reevaluate all of this in the morning."

They walked back into Addie's cabin. But suddenly, it didn't feel safe as it once had.

Even though Hayes had said everything was clear, Addie had a hard time believing him. Danger seemed to lurk everywhere.

Someone had been inside. But why?

Nothing seemed to be touched or moved.

Her laptop was sitting on the kitchen table just where she'd left it.

As Hayes double-checked all the windows, she gravitated toward her computer and clicked on the screen.

"You haven't heard back from your friend yet,

right?" she asked as she stared at her screen. "Nothing about Danielle?"

"No, not yet." He checked another window and frowned. "I'll let you know as soon as I do."

She quickly scanned her emails, but she wasn't sure what she was hoping to find. She supposed she mostly wanted something to distract herself with.

On a whim, she checked her social media also.

What she saw there caused her to suck in her breath.

"Addie?"

She pointed at the computer. "Brianna accepted my friend request."

# TWENTY-EIGHT

HAYES MADE breakfast again the next morning.

Today, the sun was brightly shining, seeming to promise the day would be full of happiness.

But in truth, he and Addie had no idea exactly what today would bring.

He only prayed there wouldn't be any more bad news.

It seemed as if they had enough of that to last a while.

Brianna had accepted Addie's friend request, but there was little on her social media to indicate what she was doing or to help them in their investigation.

There had been a few recent pictures of Brianna and Bruce here at the lake. But anyone with access to her accounts could have left them there. Someone else could have even accepted Addie's friend request.

He put some huckleberry muffins in the oven and then finished cooking the rest of the bacon. If they had to stay here much longer, they might have to look into getting more groceries.

His breath caught when Addie walked into the room.

Almost two years of marriage, and nothing had changed his attraction to her. In fact, their anniversary was in two days. Hard to believe they might spend it so close together . . . yet so far apart.

Maybe they were making progress. Maybe the truth was slowly leaking out.

He remembered her words from yesterday: *It started off with text messages like the ones you saw. But it progressed quickly. I'm pretty sure someone has been going in and out of the house as he pleases.*

His hands fisted at the thought. What else had this guy done?

He took several deep breaths, trying to concentrate on what he could control.

His only hope was that, once everything was in the open, maybe he and Addie could really work at some type of restoration.

Hayes didn't want to be foolish in his hopes or set himself up for more heartbreak.

But that was his sincere prayer.

"Look at you . . ." Addie paused near the breakfast counter. "Who knew you were a chef? You never liked cooking when we were together."

"I wouldn't call myself a chef." He shrugged. "But I can make do with what I find, I suppose. You were always a better cook, though, and I didn't mind cleaning. It seemed like a fair tradeoff."

Hayes set a plate in front of her, and she thanked him then they prayed. Small talk resumed as they asked each other questions about how they slept and discussed the weather.

She glanced outside and sobered. "Have you seen Bruce?"

He knew that question would come up.

He *had* been watching the cabin for most of the night. But it was dark, so someone could have slipped by.

"I haven't seen any signs of movement yet," Hayes said before taking a sip of his coffee. "I'm assuming he didn't stay out on the lake all night and that he came back at some point. But if he did, he was quiet. I didn't see or hear anything."

"I still can't figure out what he might have been doing." Addie absently turned the pages of a cookbook she'd brought with her.

"Your guess is as good as mine." He paused. "Did you happen to check your social media this morning? Any response from Brianna?"

"I checked. I didn't see anything else. Do you think that was really her?"

Hayes shrugged. "It's hard to say. I suppose someone else could've logged onto her account and accepted your friendship to you to throw us off. Or Brianna could truly be okay. The deputy did say he talked to her via video call."

Addie nibbled on her bottom lip as she did when she was deep in thought. "I just don't even know what to think anymore."

"Let's start by eating." He nodded at her food. "Then we'll figure out the plan for the rest of the day. Because we can't keep doing this."

As the words left his mouth, he wasn't sure if he was talking about the investigation or about his relationship with Addie.

Then Addie sucked in a breath.

She stared at a page inside the cookbook.

Hayes leaned closer to see what she was looking at.

A picture of Amy lay there—one of her and Addie smiling together at last year's Christmas party.

She turned another page.

She found an old picture of Chip swinging on a playset while Addie stood behind him.

As she kept flipping, a picture of Hayes appeared. One of them on their honeymoon.

His heart pounded harder.

"Did you leave those there?" Hayes asked, even though he already knew the answer.

Addie shook her head, her hand suddenly quaking. "No."

It suddenly became clear what someone had been doing inside the cabin earlier.

———

Addie wished she could enjoy the breakfast Hayes had made.

But she couldn't.

Not after seeing those photos.

Photos that The Guardian had obviously taken from her house.

He was here.

There was no doubt about that now.

"Anything about Danielle?" she asked as her friend's image filled her mind.

He frowned and shook his head. "Not that I've heard."

Addie's thoughts wouldn't stop racing. She had too much on her mind, she supposed.

When they finished eating and had cleaned up, Hayes turned to her, and she could tell something was on his mind.

"I'd like to hike back into the woods," he announced. "I want to get a better look at wherever it was Bruce was heading to last night."

Addie's breath caught. Those words were like magic to her ears. "That sounds like a good idea."

"Let's get changed and get going," Hayes said.

Fifteen minutes later, they were out the door. They walked the long way around through the woods, hoping that if Bruce was at his cabin, he wouldn't see them.

But everything was quiet and still over at the rental.

More questions raced through Addie's head.

Mostly, they were quiet as they headed into the wilderness.

Finally, they reached the area where they had seen Bruce near the shore last night.

As they paused and looked around, Addie sucked in a breath.

A body lay sprawled near the edge of the water.

One that had been burned beyond recognition.

HAYES PUSHED Addie back as he stared at the body.

Whoever that was . . . he couldn't identify the person. Couldn't identify if it was a male or a female.

Was Bruce connected with this?

"It's Brianna." Addie's voice cracked. "It has to be!"

He turned toward her and saw the stress on her face. The next instant, he pulled her into his arms.

She didn't resist.

In fact, she leaned into him, and he wrapped his arms tighter around her.

The two of them just fit together, almost like two pieces of a puzzle.

He relished the moment while it lasted.

"What are we going to do?" she murmured into his chest.

Hayes scanned the area around them again. There was a chance that whoever had done this was still close. They could only assume it was Bruce, but they didn't know that for sure. Until they had more answers, they needed to remain on guard.

He pulled out his phone and held it up. But he still had no cell phone service here.

"Let's get back to the cabin," he said. "We'll figure out something there."

"We can't just leave the body," she muttered.

"Right now, we don't have much choice." He took a couple of pictures with his camera phone, just in case. "I can always email these to the sheriff."

Then he glanced around, looking for other potential evidence.

He saw nothing.

Then a stick cracked in the distance.

"Did you hear that too?" Addie's voice sounded at just above a whisper.

The person who'd left this body . . . they were still close, weren't they?

Tension threaded his muscles.

"We've got to get out of here." Hayes slipped his arm around Addie's waist as he led her away. "Now."

The sooner he got her somewhere safe, the better.

Because something shady was going on here, to say the least.

———

Addie glanced around as they headed back toward the cabin. Someone was out there.

Watching them.

This person knew they'd seen the body.

What if they came after them? What if Addie or Hayes was their next victim?

Fear tried to grip her.

She couldn't let it.

Not if she wanted to survive right now.

An image of the dead body slammed into her mind again.

What happened to that person? Had he or she been burned alive? Had he or she been killed and then burned to destroy any evidence possibly left on them?

That corpse had to be Brianna. It was the only thing that made sense.

Maybe Bruce had kept her alive at first under the watchful supervision of someone else. Maybe that was why she'd been able to answer the phone when the sheriff's deputy had asked Bruce about her.

Then maybe Bruce had killed her later.

Nausea swelled in Addie's gut.

This was horrible. Maybe she should have acted quicker. Been more decisive. Bolder.

But was that even possible? As soon as she'd noticed something was wrong, she'd called Hayes. But Brianna had disappeared before she could do anything.

What if she'd confronted Bruce that night instead of running away?

But she knew the answer to that question. She would most likely be dead right now if she'd done that.

Somehow, the thought didn't make her feel any better, though.

"It's okay." Hayes's voice pulled her from her thoughts.

Addie snapped back to reality. "Nothing feels okay."

"You tried your hardest."

Again, it was like he could read her thoughts. "I just can't imagine what that person may have gone through before he or she died."

"It's better if you don't imagine it." Hayes paused a moment. "I'm liking you being here less and less all the time."

The truth was that there was nowhere she was safe. At least here, she was with Hayes.

"If Brianna's dead and the police arrest Bruce, then I'm okay leaving. Not that I want her to be dead. Don't get me wrong. I just mean if there's nothing else I can do to help—"

"I know what you're trying to say." He rubbed her arms.

Addie shut her mouth before trying to explain herself any more than necessary.

A few minutes later, the two of them emerged from the woods and began walking along the road back toward the cabin.

As they did, a car headed their way, and they paused.

The driver could be someone who could help them . . . or the driver could be trouble.

Addie watched as the vehicle pulled to a stop in front of Bruce's cabin.

A moment later, Brianna stepped out.

# CHAPTER
# THIRTY

HAYES PAUSED near the cabins and stared at the woman.

Brianna was back.

She wasn't dead.

But if she was here then . . . whose body was that back in the woods?

A grin lit the woman's face as she stepped toward Addie. "You're still here. I forgot to ask you how long you were staying. I got your friend request online and almost messaged you."

Her gaze drifted to Hayes, and he quickly introduced himself.

Addie rubbed her arms, looking as uneasy as Hayes felt.

"I thought you'd already headed home," Addie said.

Brianna shook her head. "No, I ran into a friend from college, and the two of us hung out. She just dropped me off. I decided to come back early. I felt a little guilty that I'd left Bruce since we were supposed to come here together."

"Understandable." Addie paused as if unsure exactly how to process that update. "It's good to see you."

"Is everything okay?" Brianna looked back and forth between Addie and Hayes. "You look like you've seen a ghost or something."

Addie and Hayes exchanged glances.

Finally, Addie turned back to Brianna. "It's a long story."

"I see." She glanced at her cabin. "Have you seen Bruce around this morning?"

Addie shook her head. "I can't say that I have."

"He's probably out fishing."

"Fishing? Does he like to do that alone?"

Brianna's cheeks flushed a moment. "Usually. I certainly don't like to do it with him. I can't think of anything more boring!"

"Oh . . . I just thought maybe he had a friend here he went with or something. I thought I saw him out there with someone the other day."

Brianna's eyes widened. "Did you? Maybe it was

another local he met. He can make friends anywhere. It makes me kind of jealous."

Just as she said that, another car started down the road.

It was the sheriff's deputy cruising by just as he'd promised.

Hayes knew they had to catch him and tell him about that body.

But this whole thing just kept getting not only stranger—but deadlier—by the moment.

———

As Brianna excused herself to go into her cabin, Addie quickly exchanged a glance with Hayes.

Could she have been this wrong? Had her gut feeling been totally off?

That was how it seemed.

Maybe Danielle would be okay too. She prayed that was the case.

After a moment of silence, Addie finally said, "I'm glad Brianna is here. That she's okay."

"Me too."

But she saw the hard set of Hayes's jaw.

He didn't like this either.

Hayes flagged the deputy down.

Deputy Clark pulled to a stop in front of them and rolled down his window. "How's it going?"

Hayes stepped closer to the vehicle. "Not good. I'm glad you're here because we just found a body."

The deputy's eyebrows shot up. "What?"

Hayes nodded. "Addie and I can take you there."

"I'm going to need you to do that." He grabbed his radio and called it in. Then he parked in the driveway leading to the cabin and stepped out, pulling on his coat.

As they wove between the trees of the forest, walking back toward the body, they filled the deputy in on what had happened.

"So you just happened to be walking out here, and you stumbled across it?" Deputy Clark moved a branch out of the way as they walked.

"That's right," Hayes said. "We were just as surprised as anyone would be."

"I can imagine. I don't know what in tarnation is going on here."

Fifteen minutes later, they reached the spot where they had found that dead body.

They all paused and stared.

The body—and all evidence of it—was gone.

HAYES STARED at the empty stretch of shoreline around the lake. "The body was just there. I promise."

He remembered the sounds he'd heard in the woods. Someone else had been there. And as soon as he and Addie had left, they'd taken the body. They'd taken the evidence.

"I saw it too." Addie stepped closer and shivered. "It was right there."

Deputy Clark glanced back at them. "How long ago did you leave it?"

"Probably less than an hour." Hayes pulled out his phone to find the pictures he'd taken. "Whoever took the body can't be that far away."

The deputy knelt down as if looking for shoeprints or drag marks. There were none.

"You sure it was right here?" Clark asked.

"I'm positive. I took a couple of pictures before we left, just in case."

"Smart thinking," Clark finally said. "I heard you were with Homeland Security."

"That's right. I've faced things like this a time or two."

Clark stood and looked at the photos. He held the phone up as if comparing the setting in the picture to the one in front of them.

Finally, he nodded and frowned. "I don't like the sight of that."

"Neither did we." Hayes's voice lost some of its friendliness. This man obviously wasn't seasoned, and they were losing time.

Deputy Clark glanced around. "But where would someone have taken the body? There are no roads near here. Unless they are planning on burying it in the woods."

"Or maybe disposing of it in the lake," Hayes said. "That's probably the quickest route to take. I heard back in the fifties the mafia used to dump bodies here because the lake was so deep that the bodies were never found."

"That's the rumor they have around here. But it seems like trouble rolled into town right about the same time that you guys did." The deputy let his words hang in the air a moment.

Hayes bristled. "What are you implying?"

"Nothing." The deputy shrugged. "Just making conversation."

Hayes pushed down the uneasy feeling growing inside him and focused on the missing body instead. "What are you going to do about this missing dead body?"

"I'll have some other guys come out here, and we'll search this area. I'm gonna need you to send me those pictures."

"Of course. Whatever you need."

But as Hayes glanced at Addie, he saw that her face had gone pale.

He prayed this event didn't set her back . . . just like the home invasion.

Because the further away she moved, the more he doubted he'd ever get her back.

———

Addie and Hayes had been instructed to stay out of the way at their cabin while the police did their thing.

Addie had no problem doing that.

As soon as they emerged from the woods and headed toward their cabin, Brianna stepped outside again. A knot of confusion formed between her eyes as she stared at them.

She rushed across the driveway and met them. "Everything okay? I saw the deputy stop by and then you guys disappeared into the woods."

"We're fine." Hayes's voice didn't offer any emotion or hint at the trouble around them. "The sheriff's department is just investigating something."

As another deputy pulled up, Hayes strode over to talk to him.

That gave Brianna and Addie a moment alone.

Addie knew she couldn't miss this opportunity. "Brianna . . . I have to ask . . . are you okay?"

The woman pointed toward herself. "Am *I* okay? What do you mean?"

"I heard you and Bruce arguing the other day and . . ." Addie wasn't sure exactly how to finish that statement.

Brianna laughed and waved a hand in the air. "Things get pretty heated between us sometimes. It's just the way things work. It's not really that big of a deal."

Addie wasn't sure if she was buying that. "But I saw the bruises on your arms . . ."

"Oh, that?" She glanced at her biceps. "It's just

because I'm clumsy. For real. I can't tell you how many door frames I've walked into, just because I'm not paying attention."

Addie had used that same excuse many times. On occasion, she could see where that might be the case. But when she put all the facts about Bruce and Brianna together, she still felt unsettled.

Addie stepped closer and lowered her voice. "I just wanted to let you know that if there's anything I can do, just let me know. Please."

"Oh, I appreciate that." Brianna waved her hand in the air again. "But Bruce and I are fine. I didn't mean to worry you."

"I guess it's just that I heard you guys arguing, and then you disappeared for a while and . . . I was thinking worst-case scenarios."

"I could see where you would do that. I'm sorry to concern you. But you don't worry about us. We're doing just fine."

As she said the words, Addie saw motion on the lake.

Her breath caught.

It was Bruce. He was back. In a rowboat.

By himself.

Did he kill the man who'd been with him last night?

She rubbed her throat as it tightened with the thought.

Then Addie braced herself for whatever might play out next.

# CHAPTER
# THIRTY-TWO

HAYES SAW the look of alarm on Addie's face.

He excused himself from his conversation with the sheriff's deputy and strode toward her. As he got closer, Bruce stepped out of a boat on the shoreline, tied it to a tree, and started toward them.

Hayes braced himself for another confrontation.

Bruce stormed up to Hayes and paused, standing a little too close.

"What's going on here?" Bruce planted his hands on his hips as he broadened his chest, clearly trying to look intimidating.

"I came across a dead body in the woods." Hayes decided not to beat around the bush.

Bruce's eyes widened. "What?"

"A dead body?" Brianna repeated, her pitch climbing in fear.

"Deputies are checking it out now."

Brianna's hand covered her mouth, which had dropped open in horror. "I can't believe this."

"You guys blame me for this too?" Bruce huffed, an accusatory look in his gaze. "First, I killed my wife, and now someone else?"

"Bruce . . ." Brianna scolded. "They were just worried about me and trying to be good neighbors."

He scowled. "You say worried. I say they're accusing us."

Brianna gasped. "Accusing *us*? What are you talking about?"

Hayes raised his hands, knowing he needed to defuse the situation. "Look, I'm not trying to start trouble. But we found a dead body in the woods near our cabins. I'd say it's a problem we all need to deal with."

"We can't argue with that." Brianna touched her husband's arm as if trying to calm him down. "I don't know what's going on around here, but I don't like it."

"How'd you find this body?" Bruce eyed them, his gaze still untrusting and his voice tinged with bitterness.

Hayes shrugged. "My wife and I like to take walks."

"Your wife?" Brianna's gaze flickered to Addie. "Wait . . . I didn't think you were married."

"It's a long story." Addie rubbed her throat as if uncomfortable.

Hayes didn't like the way her statement sounded, but he pushed down the emotions. He also didn't like how the tables seemed to be turning, and Bruce and Brianna were acting like he and Addie were the ones who couldn't be trusted.

"We saw you launch a boat yesterday from the same area where that body was found." Hayes decided not to hold back. "Could you explain that?"

Bruce's eyes narrowed. "I like to fish near sunset, and it's easier to launch my boat from there. Nothing illegal about it. Any more questions, Sherlock?"

Right now, Hayes really just wanted to get away from this couple. He was certain that neither of them would open up with the truth anyway.

He had no idea what exactly was going on between them, but he didn't like the situation. And he didn't like that Addie was in the middle of it.

He took Addie's hand and tugged her back. "We're going to go grab some lunch. But I'm sure we'll be seeing you around later."

Before Bruce and Brianna could say anything else, he led Addie back to the cabin and shut the door.

They needed to recalculate their next move.

But Brianna showing up had thrown a real curveball.

———

Addie's mind still raced as she and Hayes began making baked potato soup together.

"So what do you think is going on?" Addie asked Hayes as she began peeling some potatoes.

"That's a good question. I don't have enough information to draw any conclusions. By the look of things, Bruce is up to something. He's sneaking off at night. Acting cagey."

"I can't believe my gut instincts were so wrong." Addie frowned as she ran the peeler across another potato. "I was sure something bad was transpiring between Bruce and Brianna."

Hayes added some olive oil to a pan. "Maybe they do have problems. Maybe your gut instincts weren't all that wrong. Maybe they were just misdirected."

"Maybe." She continued peeling and washing the potatoes.

"Let's think this through. You were getting text messages before you saw them fighting, right?"

"That's right."

"Then we found the burned remains of someone

—remains that then disappeared. That makes it clear that someone has been watching us. Then there was the message spray-painted on the cabin, the wet footprints we saw inside, and those photos that were planted in your cookbook." He paused and shook his head. "I could take you to Vanishing Ranch. I'd feel better if you were there."

As tempting as it was, Addie knew that couldn't happen.

She realized just how sad she'd be when she and Hayes parted ways again.

She hadn't thought this experience would draw them closer. That it would bring him back into her life.

She'd missed him so much.

If they walked away from each other again, Addie knew that would be it.

Her heart panged with sadness.

Hayes seemed to forget about the onions and carrots he was sautéing in the pan and crossed his arms as he turned to her. "Addie . . . why don't you tell me the whole story? I know I've asked you that a million times. Maybe I should stop trying. I don't know anymore. I just wish I wasn't in the dark here."

"I did tell you," she started. "I told you that—"

He stepped closer and lowered his voice. "I know there's more to it."

Jitters rose inside of her.

"Why would you say that?" But she didn't sound convincing, even to her own ears.

His hands went to his hips as he stared down at her, his expression stony. "How long are you going to play this game?"

"It's not a game." Her throat felt raw as she said the words.

"Then what is it? I've tried everything I can to earn your trust back, and it never works. I'm all out of ideas. I don't even know what I did to lose your trust."

Guilt flooded her when she heard the pain in Hayes's voice. But she had to stay strong. "I told you from the start that we were over. While that sounds horrible to say, maybe the fact that you're out of ideas is the best thing in this situation. You can move on. Go back to Vanishing Ranch."

Addie felt gutted as she said those words. They pained her. But she had no choice.

"Look me in the eye and tell me you don't love me." Hayes stared at her.

Her insides quivered. He couldn't ask her to do this . . . but he was.

Was she strong enough to pull this off? To sell her story? To convince Hayes of this lie?

"Do it," Hayes muttered. "If you can say that, then I'll leave you alone. I won't ask you anymore."

This was it. Her chance to end this. To protect Hayes.

She lifted her chin. Her throat burned as she poised herself to say the words.

Finally, their gazes met.

She drew every ounce of strength inside her as she said, "I don't love you anymore, Hayes."

Nausea rose inside her. She was going to be sick. To throw up. To die of heartbreak.

But it was over. She'd done it.

As Hayes stared at her another moment, Addie saw something disappear from his gaze.

Hope.

Hope had disappeared.

It was like a door closed, and he'd realized that this was it. That their split was final.

Wasn't this what Addie wanted?

Sorrow pressed on her as the question lingered in her mind.

Because she knew the answer was a definite no.

HAYES WAS quiet as he continued to help fix dinner.

He was quiet as they ate dinner.

He was quiet as they cleaned up afterward.

Quiet as they watched the sun set and darkness descend outside.

Undeniable tension stretched between him and Addie.

But he supposed there had to come a point where he accepted her decision for what it was. He'd been in denial for far too long now.

Even though he'd always believed that marriage should be for life and that he meant it when he said till death do us part, he couldn't control Addie. She was her own person making her own choices.

He'd done everything within his power to make things work. He didn't know what else he could do.

That didn't stop the surge of anger from rushing through him.

It wasn't supposed to be this way.

Besides . . . Hayes had told her he'd leave her alone if she said those words.

He thought he'd seen lingering pain in her gaze.

But he needed to stay true to his word. He needed to leave her alone.

As soon as their tires were replaced, they needed to get away from this cabin. Once he knew she was somewhere safe, he'd wait for his and Addie's lawyers to work out their legal issues. Then he'd watch as Addie moved on.

He had to come to peace with the fact that there were some things in life he couldn't change. Addie's decision was one of those.

But that didn't change the truth that his heart felt heavy and burdened.

And broken.

It had been broken for the past four months. Until now he'd thought that maybe, just maybe, it could be mended.

But that hope had been foolish.

As Addie got up to stretch, she paced to the window and looked out. The sheriff had left probably thirty minutes ago. They hadn't found the body but promised to continue patrolling the area.

Hayes cast his other thoughts aside for a moment. "What are you looking at?"

"I know I probably sound like a broken record, but . . . I just saw someone run into the woods."

Hayes rose. "Again? Where?"

She pointed. "Over there. The same direction we saw Bruce disappear last night."

"You're sure?"

She looked up at him and nodded. "I'm positive."

"I'm going to end this once and for all." Hayes grabbed his coat and gun and strode toward the door. "Stay in here and lock the doors."

His voice left no room for argument as he headed into the darkness.

———

Addie felt sick to her stomach as she stood looking out the window.

Hayes had disappeared into the darkness outside, and she had no idea what he would be facing.

Would he track this person down? Then what would happen? Would there be a shootout or something equally as horrible?

More nausea rose inside of her.

This was getting worse and worse. Maybe she shouldn't have said anything.

She knew that Hayes was the type to run toward danger instead of away from it.

It was one of the many reasons she loved him.

Present tense. She *still* loved him.

She knew that would never change.

Addie considered telling Hayes the truth about everything. But the cost was too high. She couldn't chance his life.

She glanced at the cabin next door and saw the lights were on.

That must mean that Bruce and Brianna were there. At least one of them.

But was Bruce the one who ran into the woods?

He made the most sense.

He had gone out there last night, after all.

But as Addie watched the cabin, she saw two silhouettes inside.

Her breath caught.

What if it wasn't Bruce out there in those woods?

Could it have been The Guardian she'd seen out there? After all, someone had left those pictures in her cookbook. He was the only one who made sense.

She reached for the door handle, feeling the urge to go outside and warn Hayes.

But she'd promised him that she would stay here.

He was a trained officer of the law. Experienced. Capable.

But he didn't have any backup with him.

Her lungs tightened.

Addie didn't know what to do.

So she closed her eyes instead and began to pray.

# CHAPTER
# THIRTY-FOUR

AS SOON AS Hayes stepped into the woods, the darkness thickened.

He paused and listened.

He'd barely seen the shadow moving between the trees. But someone was out there, just as Addie had said.

What direction had this person gone?

Using the light from his cell phone, he glanced down. Even though the ground was slightly wet, he didn't see any footprints.

He heard movement in the distance.

Whoever that man was, he was on the run.

Hayes took off after him, determined to catch this guy and to get some answers.

When he had answers, he could move on. Get

away from this place. Put some space between him and Addie and deal with his heartbreak.

As the man's footsteps became faster, Hayes shouted, "Hey!"

He pushed himself to move more quickly.

But as his foot came down on the ground, he heard a snap and horrible pain bit into his leg.

He stumbled to a halt and glanced down. Metal jaws had clamped around his shin and calf.

His breath caught.

He'd stepped into a bear trap . . . most likely one that had been left here just for him.

———

Addie stayed at the window.

Was that a yell? She thought for sure she'd heard something.

Had it been Hayes? Was he okay?

The questions raced through her head.

Something was wrong.

She could feel it in her bones.

She gripped the door handle again as she contemplated her options.

What if he was hurt? What if he needed her help?

Or what if that sound had just been a ruse? What if someone was trying to lure her outside?

And what about her promise to Hayes?

Then again, Addie had promised to love him until death. And she *did* love him.

Everything was just so complicated.

She waited, hardly breathing. She didn't want to miss a thing. Didn't want to miss a sound.

"Come on . . ." she muttered, still staring outside. "If something's wrong, I need to know. Please, God."

That's when she heard another yell.

The sound of it sealed her decision.

She was going out there.

She slipped on her coat and rushed outside.

She followed the path Hayes had taken into the woods.

Once she slipped between the trees, she kept running.

She had to find him.

What if he was hurt because of her? It would be all her fault. She'd brought Hayes into this.

"Hayes?" she called.

She paused but heard nothing.

Where was he?

Addie took several more steps, deeper into the woods. She prayed she didn't get lost. Prayed she didn't wander into some kind of trap.

After running several more feet, she paused again

and looked around. She fought the panic that tried to set in.

"Hayes?" she called.

"Over . . . here," a deep, strained voice said.

Her lungs froze.

Was that Hayes?

"It's me," he said as if reading her mind. "Addie . . . I'm . . . I'm hurt."

At his words, her heart sank.

She darted toward him, still not seeing him in the dark. She should've brought a flashlight—or her phone so she could use the flashlight app. But she hadn't been thinking. Only reacting.

A few steps later, she nearly tripped over him.

He lay on the ground. Grasping his leg.

He shone a light on his calf, and that's when Addie saw the bear trap clamping his leg. Saw his torn, blood-soaked jeans.

Her head began to spin. "Oh, Hayes . . ."

"I need to get this off." His voice sounded urgent. "I'm gonna need your help."

"I'm not sure what I can do." Her heart thumped harder. She didn't have experience with this sort of thing. From what she'd heard, bear traps weren't easy to get undone.

"I can talk you through it. We just need to push this trap open far enough that I can slip my leg out."

Her heart thumped in her ears. "Is your leg broken?"

"I don't think so." He shifted, his face twisted with pain. "Now, I need you to find two big sticks. I need you to wedge them in the trap and then pull them in opposite directions. Hopefully, the leverage will be enough to pry it open enough to let me get my leg out. Can you do that?"

Addie nodded.

She would do anything for Hayes.

Anything except stay married.

THE PERSON who'd set this trap was probably still close by. He might even be watching this. Enjoying the show.

Hayes tried not to give away just how much pain he was in. He didn't want to freak out Addie, and he didn't want whoever did this to have the satisfaction of seeing him suffer.

"Don't go too far," Hayes warned Addie. "Stay within eyesight."

He had his gun at his side, and he could still shoot with the best of them.

But it was dark out here. Hard to see.

A few minutes later, Addie returned with something in hand. "I found some fallen branches. I think these will work."

He shone his flashlight on his leg so she could see

better. "Okay, wedge them in between the jaws of the trap. Whatever you do, don't let your fingers or hands or anything else get in between these claws. Understand?"

She nodded, fear filling her eyes. "I understand."

Working quickly, she did as he said. Then, with a grunt, she leveraged the two sticks. She gritted her teeth as she used every ounce of strength she had to force the contraption open.

Just as Hayes hoped, the motion offered him just enough relief that he could pull his leg out.

When he was free, Addie released her hold and the trap clamped down on the branches with a loud snap.

His pants were shredded, and blood ran down his leg.

But things could have been so much worse.

At least he could move.

Addie stared at him with wide eyes as her shallow breaths came entirely too frequently. "Can you walk?"

Hayes stood and tried to put some weight on his leg.

As he did, he winced with pain.

Instinctively, Addie slipped her arm around him and helped hold him up.

After a moment, he got his balance. "I think I'll be okay. I just have to take it slow."

"I can help with that. I'll go as slowly as you need to."

The irony of Addie's words hit him.

That's what he'd told her when they first started dating. When he learned about the abusive relationship she'd been in. Hayes hadn't wanted to push her too hard.

Now here she was saying the same words to him.

Carefully, they walked back through the forest toward the cabin. As they did, he glanced around, looking for signs of anyone who might be watching or waiting to attack.

Hayes saw no one.

But that didn't mean that someone wasn't out there.

That person had to be somewhere nearby.

Finally, they reached the cabin, and Addie helped him inside.

But they weren't out of danger yet.

———

Addie helped Hayes to the couch and didn't release him until he was lying down with his leg raised.

"I think there's a first aid kit around here somewhere," she murmured. "I'll be right back. I'll also grab some towels and wet washcloths."

Addie quickly scrambled away, her mind nearly frantic.

She found what she needed and rushed back to him.

But she didn't like how pale he was becoming.

What if he lost too much blood? She had no transportation. No phone signal.

How would she get him help?

She supposed she could go next door and ask to borrow either Bruce or Brianna's vehicle. But she still wasn't sure if she could trust Bruce.

The questions rushed through her head.

Right now, she just needed to focus on Hayes. "I'm going to need to pull your pant leg up so I can see the damage."

Hayes pressed his eyes closed before nodding. "Of course. I think it just cut my calf. I don't think it broke a bone. Thankfully, it was just a small bear trap."

A small bear trap? It was still a bear trap.

This was serious.

But Addie didn't say that aloud.

She swallowed hard before asking, "Do you think somebody set it up intending for you to step on it?"

"I do. He led me right to it."

His words caused another shot of fear to rush through her.

Carefully raising his pants leg, she stared at the gaping wound on his calf.

She stifled a gasp.

This wasn't good.

She put a towel underneath his leg and then wet a washcloth with warm water and began to gently clean the wounds. When she finished, she took some antibiotic cream and gently dabbed it on him.

Addie felt woozy looking at it, but she forced herself to do it anyway. She had to know what the damage was.

The cuts weren't quite as deep as she thought they might be.

That was good news, at least.

She studied the wounds another moment. "I'm not sure if you need stitches."

"It probably wouldn't hurt."

"For now, I'm going to wrap your leg with gauze. I think the bleeding is stopping. That's good."

Addie dressed and bandaged Hayes's wound carefully, trying not to bring him any more pain.

She added medical tape to secure it all in place and then leaned back, trying to catch her breath.

She still couldn't believe that this had just happened.

What if that bear trap had broken his leg? Or what if someone had been there waiting with a gun to finish him off once he was down?

Emotion welled in her chest.

She'd tried to do everything that man had told her to do, and Hayes was still suffering.

Anger and frustration mounted.

What was she supposed to do now?

WHEN HAYES LOOKED at Addie and saw the concern on her face, realization filled him.

She still cared about him.

He had no doubt about that at this very moment.

Even though she'd been shaken, she'd done a great job bandaging his wound.

Hayes had told her the truth when he said he might need stitches. But based on his experience, it could go either way.

He was just thankful that the trap hadn't bit into his leg any deeper. That his boot had caught part of it.

"Addie . . ." he murmured, trying to get her attention before she went into shock.

Her face looked so pale, and her breathing was entirely too shallow.

As Addie glanced at him, she nearly collapsed onto the floor.

He sat up, catching her. As he pulled her into a hug, she began to sob.

"I'm so sorry," she muttered into his chest. "I'm so sorry."

"What are you sorry about?" he murmured into her hair.

"Everything. There's just so much to this."

He stroked her back as he tried to comfort her, as he tried to understand. "I'm not sure what that means."

She pulled away from him, her eyes watery and red-rimmed as her gaze connected with his. "I thought you were going to die."

She was so confusing—one minute acting as if she cared and the next as if she wanted nothing to do with him. But Hayes wasn't going to put a kibosh on this conversation.

"You didn't lose me," he told her softly. "I'm right here."

"All I ever wanted to do was protect you."

He froze a moment, unsure if he'd heard correctly. "What does that mean? You wanted to protect me?"

Addie pulled away, and their gazes met. The next instant, she pressed her lips into his.

Hayes stiffened, but only for a second.

Then he wrapped his arms around her and held her closer as the kiss deepened.

———

Addie didn't know what she was doing. Perhaps she was following her heart and forgetting about all the rules The Guardian had given her.

But none of that mattered anymore.

All that mattered was Hayes. That he was okay.

It didn't take long for her to remember the familiarity of his lips.

The months of frustration, agony, and heartbreak had built a tension and pressure between them that was all released in this kiss.

Until Hayes pulled away, questions in his eyes. His gaze searched hers for answers.

"Addie . . . I want nothing more than to continue this . . . but . . ."

She rocked back, resisting the urge to touch her lips. To close her eyes and pretend like it hadn't ended.

This wasn't fair to Hayes. She knew it wasn't.

"What did you mean when you said you only wanted to protect me?" Hayes's gaze locked with hers.

This was it. The moment Addie had to decide

whether to keep going with her charade or to own up to the whole truth.

Addie had gone no contact as instructed, and Hayes had still almost died.

What if she was breaking his heart for nothing?

"Addie . . ." Hayes gently prodded.

She grabbed his hand and pressed her forehead into it as her thoughts raced.

Tension pulsed inside her, followed by nausea.

She only wanted to do the right thing. But what that right thing was felt murky right now.

"Hayes . . . I love you so much," she started. "I've always loved you, and nothing will ever change that."

"Then why . . . ?"

"He said he would kill you if I didn't leave you," she blurted.

Addie wasn't sure if saying the words aloud made her feel relief or more panic.

The jury was still out.

Hayes straightened. "Wait. Who said that?"

She shook her head. "I don't know who. He calls himself The Guardian. He sent me pictures of you with a target on your back. Said he could plant a bomb in your car, or have a sniper shoot you, or poison you even. He seemed to have thought everything out. He wanted to let me know he was serious. I had no doubt about that."

"What?"

"Then he was hiding in the backseat of my car one day." She swallowed hard. "He wanted to let me know he wasn't playing. Before he left, he pressed his cigarette into my back."

She tugged the collar of her shirt down enough to show him the scar on her upper back.

"No . . ." Hayes muttered.

She let go of her shirt and nodded.

"Oh, Addie . . ."

It took every ounce of her energy to keep her cool right now.

"Then he showed me a video of you being shot at while you were in Houston working a case. He was the one holding the gun. Everyone thought it was one of your suspects."

"What? He was the one who did that? We thought it was the cartel."

She nodded, her throat burning. "He made it clear that he was serious. If I stayed with you . . . he was going to kill you, and there was nothing I could do to stop it. He said next time you wouldn't be so lucky."

"Are you saying . . . you asked me to leave because someone threatened you?" Pain stretched through his voice.

Addie leaned toward him, trying to make him realize how serious this was. "No, Hayes. Someone threatened to kill *you*. This guy meant it. He told me what he was going to do to you. I couldn't let that happen. Not after everything you'd done for me."

Hayes tilted his head, compassion welling in his gaze. "Addie . . . I don't even know what to say."

"You saved me. You showed me how good a man could be. What it felt like to be treated with respect and love." Her voice cracked. "I knew breaking up with you might hurt, but it was better than you being dead. I love you too much for that."

"I love you too. Always." Hayes lifted her chin, and his hand cupped her cheek. "But Addie, if you had told me, I could've helped you work through it. Did you ever think about that?"

She wiped the tears that flooded from her eyes. "Of course, I thought about it. I thought about it every day! I wasn't sure if what I was doing was right or not. I only knew I couldn't let anything happen to you."

"Addie . . ." Hayes threw his head back as if he couldn't believe this conversation.

"I'm sorry," she murmured again. "I'm so, so sorry."

Her mom was right.

She did ruin everything.

# THIRTY-SEVEN

HAYES COULDN'T BELIEVE what Addie was telling him.

*That* was the reason she asked for a divorce?

Why hadn't she trusted him enough to tell him what was going on?

Or, in her head, had she truly broken up with him out of a place of love?

It was so against anything he'd ever assumed.

In fact, Hayes didn't know what to think about it.

Part of him was angry. They could have cleared this up with a conversation.

But he knew the situation ran deeper than that with Addie, especially since she had experienced so much pain during her first marriage.

Addie had experienced abuse firsthand, and now she wanted to protect others from similar hurt.

If only they could go back in time . . . if they could've done things differently. If Hayes knew then what he knew now.

In truth, this started before her disastrous first marriage. It started when her brother had been killed by that car. Her guilt had compounded over the years.

But Hayes truly believed in a God who was capable of changing lives. He knew Addie would always hold that pain, but that she could use it for good. That God could turn things around.

But that home invasion had triggered something inside her, hadn't it?

"Can I see the messages?" he asked quietly, still reeling over her words.

Addie nodded, grabbed her phone, and handed it to him.

The sick feeling churned harder in his stomach with each message he read. With each picture he saw.

He could see why Addie thought this guy was serious.

Because he was.

"Do you hate me?" Addie stared at him with questions in her gaze.

"I could never hate you." He reached up until his fingers tangled with her hair. "Never. Come here."

She curled onto the couch beside him.

He pulled her into his arms.

Hayes had a lot that he needed to think about right now.

A lot.

But he knew one thing for certain.

His hope was back in full force.

---

Addie relished the feel of Hayes's arms around her. Oh, how she had missed this. How she had missed him.

But she'd be foolish if she thought one conversation had cleared up all their problems.

She knew it didn't. Their issues ran deeper than that.

They'd been apart for four months.

But for now, she appreciated the warmth of Hayes's body heat as they held each other.

She worried about his injury to his leg. The cut could've been so much deeper than it was. Still, if infection set in . . .

He needed to have the wound checked out.

As her thoughts raced, Hayes remained quiet as if lost in his own thoughts.

Was whatever was happening between Bruce and Brianna somehow connected with her past?

Her friend had let her use this cabin. Was it possible that The Guardian had tracked Geraldo and Julia down and found out her plans? Had he then followed her here?

It was a possibility.

Nothing was making sense. But someone clearly wanted to scare them. To hurt them.

Addie needed to figure out what she was going to do about it.

HAYES LAY ON THE COUCH, but he couldn't sleep. He had too much on his mind.

Starting with Addie.

He wanted to believe they'd turned a corner. And maybe they had. But he also realized their kiss didn't really solve anything, that they had other issues.

Their problems were far from being over.

For now, Hayes tried to enjoy the moment. He wrapped his arms more tightly around Addie and held her close. The scent of her cotton-scented shampoo lifted up to him, and he closed his eyes, relishing the aroma a moment.

He'd dreamed about reconciliation for so long. Dreamed about what it would be like to hold Addie again. To have another chance.

Maybe that's what they were being given.

Before he could think about it too long, a noise caught his ear, and he stiffened.

Someone had shouted in the distance.

The only place that could have come from would be Bruce and Brianna's cabin.

Addie seemed to hear it too, and she went still.

Hayes pushed himself up on the couch, ignoring the ache in his leg.

Addie looked up at him. "Who was that?"

"I'm not sure." He pulled away so he could listen better.

That's when he heard a slam and another shout.

Something was going on over at Bruce and Brianna's place.

He pushed himself to a standing position, pausing for long enough to get his balance.

His leg still hurt, but he could put weight on it.

He grabbed his coat along with his gun and a flashlight.

"What are you doing?" Addie stood, her wide eyes on him.

"I have to see what's going on."

"But . . ."

"If Brianna is hurt, I need to know." Hayes locked gazes with her. "You called me for help. That's what I'm going to do."

She stared at him another moment before nodding. "Be careful."

"Stay here." His voice left no room for argument.

Then he stepped outside to see what was happening.

———

Addie had to do something besides wait and worry.

So she pulled out her cookie dough and added some chocolate chips. She wouldn't bake the cookies right now. But maybe later.

If she survived long enough to do so.

What was happening out there?

She knew it was better if she stayed inside right now just in case things turned south.

But Hayes was injured, and he was out there alone.

She finally abandoned the cookie dough.

She grabbed her phone and held it up, looking for a signal.

There was none.

Of course.

Instead, she sat at the computer. Maybe she could check her emails. Maybe there was an update on Danielle.

She still held out hope that her friend was okay.

She prayed that was the case.

But there were no updates.

Her gaze stopped on another message, this one from a trainer at the gym.

"I've been trying to get in touch with Geraldo and Julia. Have you talked to them?"

Addie's heart pounded harder.

Geraldo and Julia owned this cabin.

They were the only people who knew exactly where she'd gone.

What if The Guardian had grabbed them and demanded they tell him where Addie had gone?

What if more people had suffered because of her?

Her head spun at the thought.

HAYES CAUTIOUSLY APPROACHED Bruce's cabin.

The front door was open.

Everything around him had gone silent.

But Bruce's truck was still out front.

What exactly had happened over here? He'd heard some kind of commotion. He was sure of it.

Gripping his gun, he crept closer.

He carefully stepped onto the deck and paced to the front door. As he knocked, it swung open wider.

His muscles bristled.

"Hello?" Hayes called, his body on guard and ready to act. "I heard some yelling, and I wanted to make sure everything was okay."

There was no answer.

Worst-case scenarios flashed through his mind.

He hoped he wouldn't find anyone dead inside. He prayed that wouldn't be the case.

He eased into the dark cabin, which was quickly becoming familiar. Using a flashlight, he shone it around.

Nothing out of the ordinary caught his eye.

Not yet.

He searched room by room.

The place was empty.

Pausing in the middle of the living room a moment, he frowned.

Where had Bruce and Brianna gone?

Were they taking another late-night trek?

Hayes stepped back outside and searched the ground. He saw two sets of footprints leading into the woods.

The good news was that there were no drag marks.

At just that moment, his cell phone buzzed.

He must have come across one of those patchy spots of service up here. He glanced at the screen and saw his old friend from Homeland Security had texted him back. He quickly read the message.

The main person Hayes had suspected might have sent Addie the threats was still behind bars. So he couldn't be behind this.

Hayes supposed that was good news.

But he'd also asked John to look into Bruce Newton.

Hayes quickly skimmed the rest of the message.

It appeared that Bruce had a criminal record for drug possession and distribution.

A new thought hit him. Could Bruce have been incarcerated at the same prison where someone Hayes had locked up was? Was that the connection they were looking for?

It was worth considering.

Hayes frowned.

He didn't like the sound of that.

He needed to call the sheriff's department while he had a signal.

He wasn't going to go through these woods looking for Bruce and Brianna himself. Because that would mean leaving Addie behind or having her go with him.

Neither option was viable.

Hayes needed to get back to Addie and get her out of here.

Now.

———

As they'd waited for the sheriff to arrive, Addie listened to Hayes's update.

She understood Hayes's reasoning for not wanting to search the woods himself. It seemed like a good decision, especially considering his injury and the bear trap he'd stumbled upon earlier.

Still, Addie was concerned about Brianna. She hoped her neighbor was okay. Had she walked into the woods with Bruce willingly? Or had he forced her to go?

As Hayes talked to the sheriff and Deputy Clark, Addie stood outside despite the cold.

She wasn't sure what she thought being out here would accomplish, but she kept staring at the woods and thinking about Brianna.

A few moments earlier, she'd heard the sheriff mention getting some dogs and sending a team out to look for Brianna and Bruce.

Apparently, more deputies from the surrounding counties were on their way also.

Needing a breather, Addie paced to the shoreline. She made sure to stay in sight of everyone. It wouldn't be safe not to. However, the area between the cabins and the water felt safe.

She stared across the glimmering lake and crossed her arms over her chest.

How could such a peaceful place attract such cruelty and violence?

How was she going to pick up the pieces of all

this when it was over? And how would this situation end?

The man taunting her seemed intent on making sure she was miserable.

Did that mean he would kill everyone she cared about?

Her heart panged at the thought.

She could run again, but what would that accomplish? Would Hayes still be a target?

And how did Bruce and Brianna tie in with this?

The questions made her head pound harder.

As she glanced back at the team behind her, a stick cracked in the distance.

Before she realized what was happening, a shadow rushed at her.

A hand covered her mouth.

An arm wrapped around her waist and lifted her off her feet.

Addie began kicking as panic raced through her.

Then someone whispered in her ear, "You should have never disobeyed me. Now you'll have to pay."

HAYES TURNED AWAY from Sheriff Liberman and glanced around.

They were about to send some deputies into the woods to look for Bruce and Brianna.

In the meantime, he searched the deck of the cabin for Addie.

She'd just been standing there, leaning on the railing with that forlorn look on her face.

Had she gone back inside? It *was* awfully cold out here.

Hayes barely heard what the sheriff was saying as he continued to survey the area for her.

Finally, he turned to Liberman and asked, "Will you excuse me for a moment?"

Liberman nodded and turned to talk to his deputies.

Hayes limped back to the cabin. He needed to know for sure that Addie was inside. Call it paranoid, but he needed confirmation. To see it with his own eyes.

Especially after everything that had happened.

He stepped inside and glanced around but didn't see her. "Addie?"

There was no answer.

A bad feeling brewed in his gut. He hoped his instincts were wrong. But something didn't feel right.

"Addie?" He strode through the cabin toward her bedroom.

He knocked and opened the door.

But no one was inside.

He checked the bathroom, but there was still no Addie.

If she wasn't inside and she wasn't on the deck, then where had she gone?

More urgency filled his steps as he went back outside.

This time, he paid closer attention to everything around him.

He saw Addie's footprints in the remaining snow.

They led off the deck.

Using his flashlight, Hayes continued to follow them.

The prints led to the shoreline—the empty shoreline.

Addie must have wandered down there to take a look at the lake. She would have still been within sight of them, so she probably hadn't thought much of it.

But where was she now?

His lungs tightened.

Hayes followed her tracks to the shore.

But when he reached the sandy beach, he saw exactly what he feared.

A second set of footprints.

This one led to the swath of woods beside him.

His heart beat harder.

He cupped his hands over his mouth as he yelled, "Addie!"

Somehow, he knew there would be no response.

---

Terror rushed through Addie.

She couldn't see the man behind her. She could only feel the knife he held at her throat as he pulled her along the uneven ground.

She instinctively knew this was the same man who'd been involved in her home invasion four months ago.

Who was he? Why was he so determined to make her life miserable?

Was it Reggie?

He was one of the only people who would have had access to some of those photos.

But he was supposed to be dead.

She didn't have time to think about that now.

Right now, she had to concentrate on survival.

The man was bigger than she was and had easily overpowered her.

He still kept the knife at her throat and an arm over her arms and chest. He had lifted her off her feet partly as he dragged her uphill and deeper into the woods. The scent of cigarettes wafted from him— reminding her of the incident in her car and the burn mark on her back.

What was this guy going to do with her? Was he going to kill her?

She dug her shoes into the ground where she could, hoping to leave marks where someone would be able to track her.

Hayes would come looking. Had he even realized she was gone? Would he be able to find her in time?

Would this guy ambush Hayes in the process?

The questions rushed through Addie's mind.

But this was the very reason she knew she

couldn't be with Hayes. She should have stuck to her guns. Should have stayed away.

Finally, the man paused at the rocky cliffs overlooking the lake.

Addie's heart pounded in her ears as she stared at the steep drop-off.

What was he going to do now?

As she stared at the water way down below, she feared she knew the answer to that question.

# CHAPTER
## FORTY-ONE

HAYES RUSHED across the rocky ground until he reached Sheriff Liberman. He told him what was going on. But he didn't wait for the sheriff to take charge.

Instead, Hayes pushed through his pain and rushed into the woods.

He had to follow those footprints. He couldn't let too much time pass. Couldn't let Addie get too far away.

The sheriff had muttered something about sending some guys to help.

But right now, all Hayes could think about was finding Addie.

With every second that passed, she could be in more danger. Hayes couldn't let that happen.

He tried to follow the footsteps for as long as he could.

He found a few places where shoes had left drag marks.

But as the steep ground became rocky, the markings disappeared.

Hayes searched for areas of vegetation that had been trampled.

But there were very few signs to show where they had gone.

Addie and the person who'd taken her could have gone farther up the mountain. Or they could have headed west and crossed the road to go into the woods there.

Hayes's lungs tightened. There were too many possibilities here.

But he'd learned long ago to listen to his gut.

He continued in the same direction he'd been going.

As he climbed farther, he paused to listen.

From here, he could still hear the sheriff's deputies coming behind him.

But the woods themselves seemed quiet.

Hayes wanted to yell for Addie. But he couldn't let himself do that. He had to assume her abductor still had her.

Instead, he kept walking, praying he would find his wife.

Not just find her—but find her alive and well.

———

"Who are you?" Addie's voice trembled as she asked the question.

"It's not important." The man pressed his knife to her throat.

She didn't know what he was planning.

But she knew her feet were dangerously close to the edge of the cliff. That one wrong move would send her toppling.

Even if she landed in the water, it was so cold that hypothermia would quickly kick in.

That was if she survived the fall.

From where she stood, she could see the many rocks along the way that could crush her body on impact.

A tremble raked through her.

When this man finished with her, would he go after Hayes?

That was the last thing she wanted.

"I was planning to kill you," the man muttered into her ear.

Cold fear rushed through her.

That voice . . . why did it sound slightly familiar? Had she heard it before?

"But then I thought it would be more fun to kill *him*," the man continued.

Addie's heart rate ratcheted.

He was talking about Hayes.

More self-doubt pummeled her. She should never have brought Hayes into this. What had she been thinking? She was going to get him killed!

"Please . . ." Her voice came out sounding strangled. "Leave us alone."

"Sorry . . . I can't do that. I made a promise."

A promise? What did that mean even?

"On second thought . . . I think I'll stick to my original plan," the man whispered in her ear before he shoved her.

Addie began falling to her death.

HAYES FROZE.

Was that a scream?

That's what it sounded like.

It had to be Addie.

He sprinted toward the noise, desperate to help. The yell sounded like it came from the north, farther up the mountain.

Cold fear rushed through him.

"Addie?" Hayes called her name this time, realizing that if she was in trouble, that nothing else mattered.

There was no response.

He kept climbing up the rocky mountain, searching for her. Keeping an eye open for trouble. Knowing that if he stepped on another bear trap, it would delay him . . . indefinitely this time.

Whoever was behind this was smart. This guy could have very well set up another scenario like that. Set another trap.

"Addie?" Hayes called again.

This time, he thought he heard someone respond.

He paused and listened.

But there was nothing.

"Where are you?" Hayes called.

Footsteps hurried in the distance. Underbrush shifted. Rocks tumbled.

Someone was running away.

Escaping.

But it was just the sound of one set of footsteps.

If that was the perpetrator running . . . then where was Addie?

"Hayes . . ." a strained voice yelled. "I'm here."

That was *definitely* Addie. She was close.

But as Hayes scanned the woods around him, he didn't see her anywhere.

"You've got to help me!" she yelled. "I don't have much time. I'm . . . slipping."

He followed her voice to the edge of the cliff and looked down, shining his flashlight.

That's when he saw Addie hanging by her fingertips from a rocky ledge.

———

Addie could feel her fingers slipping.

She didn't know how much longer she could hold on.

But at least she was still alive.

When she saw Hayes's face above her, momentary relief rushed through her.

He was here. He could help.

But what if that man came back? What if he tried to finish what he started? If he acted on his plan to kill Hayes too?

She didn't know what was going on with that guy.

She only knew that if she let go of this ledge, she'd plunge to her death.

"Addie . . . I'm going to help you," Hayes muttered.

He lowered himself to his stomach and reached for her. But his arms weren't long enough. She was too far down.

More fear pulsed through her—both for herself and for Hayes.

"Hayes . . . you've got to be careful."

"We just need to worry about you right now," he told her.

"The ledge . . . it's not stable. You can't climb down here."

"I'm not leaving you."

Addie appreciated that sentiment.

But she didn't see how this was going to work.

"Can you find a foothold?" Hayes asked.

"I already tried. There's nothing within reach."

Her muscles cramped, and one of her hands started to slip.

She clamped harder, determined not to die this way. She'd fight with everything inside her.

She glanced back at Hayes, knowing his eyes would bring her hope.

But as she looked up at him, a shadow shifted behind him.

That man . . . he was back.

Panic raced through her.

"Hayes!" she shouted. "Behind you."

Addie prayed her words hadn't come too late.

# CHAPTER
# FORTY-THREE

HAYES TURNED in time to see a masked man standing over him.

The man held a large rock over his head.

He was going to slam that into Hayes, wasn't he?

As the man threw his arms down, Hayes quickly rolled out of the way.

The rock slammed into the ground.

Hard.

The masked man grunted.

Hayes hopped to his feet and crouched in fight mode.

Suddenly, he wasn't thinking about his leg. Survival was all that mattered.

Because if he died, Addie would die too.

He only prayed the sheriff and his deputies had heard the commotion and were close.

The man grabbed the rock again and growled as he turned back toward Hayes.

Hayes braced himself.

In one motion, the man raised the huge rock over his head again and catapulted it toward Hayes.

Hayes ducked.

As he did, he charged at the man's knees.

The man fell back.

With the wind temporarily knocked out of the man, Hayes reached for the man's mask to see who this was once and for all.

Before he could grasp it, Addie shouted, "Hayes!"

She was about to fall, wasn't she?

Hayes stared at the man again. He didn't want to let him get away.

This was his chance to find answers.

But he had to make a choice.

That choice was clearly going to be Addie.

The man seemed to sense that.

He scrambled back and took off in a run.

Hayes wanted to chase the man, but he couldn't.

Instead, he rushed back toward the cliff and glanced down.

His heart skipped a beat when he saw Addie dangling by only one hand now.

She didn't have much time.

Hayes had to act.

Now.

———

Addie wanted to hear Hayes's voice.

Wanted to know that he was okay.

For a moment, she forgot her own perilous situation.

All she could think about was Hayes.

She'd heard the grunts above her. Heard rocks hitting the ground. Several pebbles had rolled down and hit her face.

She knew she shouldn't, but she glanced beneath her.

The moonlight displayed the sparkling water taunting from below.

Would the lake she'd always dreamed about visiting become her grave?

Of all the ways she'd seen herself dying, this wasn't one of them.

"I'm going to get you." Hayes appeared above her again.

Relief washed through her. "You're okay?"

"I'm okay. I'm here. Just hold on a couple more minutes. You can do it."

More scrambling and shouts sounded from above.

Addie didn't think it was the man coming back.

No, more than one person was heading this way.

Then she heard a familiar voice.

It was the sheriff, she realized.

He and his men were here to help.

"I need you to hold onto me," Hayes shouted to someone behind him.

"No, we can get a crew here to help—" someone else said.

"We don't have time for that," Hayes said. "Hold onto my legs and lower me so I can grab her."

As he said the words, another rock on the ledge Addie held onto slipped, plummeting to the water below.

She knew her time was running out.

Fear shuddered through her at the thought.

WITH DEPUTIES HOLDING onto each of his legs, Hayes lowered himself toward Addie. He just needed to grab her wrist. Then he could pull her up.

The situation wasn't ideal. But they had to make do with what they had. Time was of the essence right now.

"I'm not letting you fall." He stretched as he reached for her.

But she was still about six inches out of his grasp.

"Hayes . . ." Addie stared up at him with her wide, terrified eyes.

He never wanted to see her look like that again. Never.

"Lower!" Hayes shouted.

The two deputies holding onto him lowered him even more.

Half of Hayes's body was now over the cliff.

If they let go of him, he'd go tumbling down and take Addie with him.

He had to trust them.

Hayes reached for her again.

This time his hand gripped her wrist.

His heart rate slowed . . . but only for a moment.

This was a good first step, but they still had farther to go.

"Can you grab my other wrist with your free hand?" he called.

Addie groaned but reached up and did as he asked.

He clamped her wrists tightly.

They were locked together solid now.

No way was he letting her go.

"Pull me up!" he yelled.

They slowly began to tug him upward. As they did, Hayes held onto Addie with an iron clamp.

She might have a bruise on her wrists in the morning, but if that was the worst injury she walked away with then she was doing well.

Finally, as they got closer to the edge, two other deputies grabbed Addie by the arms. They hauled her to the top of the cliff, where she collapsed onto the ground.

Hayes crawled over to her and threw his arms around her.

Addie was safe.

But that had been close.

Too close.

Next time, this guy might be successful.

Hayes couldn't let there be a next time.

———

Thirty minutes later, Addie was sitting in the back of an ambulance, and paramedics were checking out her injuries.

All things considered, she had nothing to complain about. Sure, she would be sore tomorrow, and she might have some bruises and cuts.

But she was alive.

So was Hayes.

Things could have turned out so much differently. If that man had been able to throw that rock onto Hayes's head . . . he wouldn't be here right now.

The Guardian had warned her before. Told her that if she didn't back away from Hayes that her husband would be killed.

He'd proven that he wasn't bluffing.

She shivered.

Had this guy been watching her all these months?

That was how it appeared.

Another shiver raked through her.

Hayes was in another ambulance, and someone was checking out the bear trap wound he'd received last night.

Addie had done all she could to treat his injury, but she felt better knowing that he could get stitches and antibiotics now if needed.

Her thoughts wandered.

All of this started because of Bruce and Brianna.

Now they were all but forgotten.

Addie frowned.

She should have never walked alone down by the shoreline.

If she hadn't, then the sheriff and his deputies could be looking for Brianna right now. Instead, they'd had to go and rescue her.

And what was she going to do about Hayes?

Her gaze traveled toward him. He looked so handsome, so in control as he chatted with the sheriff in the back of the ambulance. Based on the way the sheriff spoke with him, there was a level of mutual respect between them.

Hayes had been good at his job. People respected him. Looked up to him.

He'd loved her, and he'd loved her well.

Yet Addie had brought him here and put him in

danger—the very danger she'd tried desperately to protect him from.

Should she break his heart again and send him away?

Would that keep him safe?

Now that he knew the truth, would he even leave?

The questions swirled in her mind.

She didn't have any good answers.

She didn't have any answers at all, for that matter.

The fact was . . . she had no idea what to do.

# CHAPTER
# FORTY-FIVE

HAYES DIDN'T WANT to go to the hospital, so he'd told the paramedics to give him stitches there.

He stared at Addie as she sat in the other ambulance. He saw the stress on her face, and he understood the place it came from.

The person who'd broken into their house four months ago had done this, hadn't he?

Hayes should have never let Addie out of his sight tonight.

The man had obviously been waiting for the right opportunity to pounce.

And he'd found it.

Things could have turned out so much differently. Hayes was thankful for this happy ending, even if it was temporary. Still, he couldn't let down his guard yet.

"Do you have any idea what's going on?" Sheriff Liberman asked.

Hayes wasn't sure how much he should say.

"I'm not sure exactly what's going on with Bruce and Brianna," Hayes finally said. "I'm truly concerned about them and worried that maybe Bruce is hurting Brianna. As far as the incident with my wife . . . all I can think of is that trouble somehow followed her here."

"Trouble in the sense of someone from your former job?" He raised an eyebrow. "You said you were Homeland Security."

Hayes's background in law enforcement made the most sense as far as singling out a suspect. But there were no cases he could think of where any of the accused would want to target Addie.

He rubbed his jaw. "I don't think that's it."

"Is there any reason someone would want to target your wife?"

That was an excellent question, Hayes mused.

"We had a break-in at our house about four months ago. Addie has been receiving some threatening texts since then. I thought someone was just blowing smoke, but maybe there's more to it than that."

Reggie was dead. Addie didn't exactly have a long list of enemies because of her exercise studio.

Why *would* someone want to target her?

Before Hayes could think about the answer to that question, he saw movement in the woods, and he braced himself.

He halfway expected a bear to emerge.

But instead, it was a person.

Bruce Newton.

And he lumbered out of the forest covered in blood.

---

Addie's gaze widened when she spotted Bruce.

What had happened to him?

Had he been attacked by a bear?

As sheriff's deputies rushed toward him, Addie glanced beyond the man. Her gaze searched the woods.

But Brianna didn't emerge.

Where was she?

Disastrous scenarios flashed through her mind.

Brianna dead. Attacked by the same bear. Left bleeding out.

Hayes hopped from the back of the ambulance, gravitating toward her. No doubt it was a protective measure.

Standing beside each other, they both watched as Bruce hobbled closer.

Two deputies and a paramedic intercepted him before he got too close.

"You've got to help me," Bruce muttered, clutching his chest as if he couldn't breathe.

"Where's your wife?" Sheriff Liberman stepped closer as the deputies grasped Bruce's arms.

"They . . . have . . . her."

Addie's heart beat harder. *They* have her?

What was Bruce talking about?

"Sir, can you be more specific?" Liberman asked. "Who has her?"

Bruce looked up with haggard, guilt-ridden eyes.

Based on the amount of blood on his shirt, he'd lost enough that he was in critical condition right now.

"Did you hear me?" Liberman's voice climbed higher. "Who has your wife? What happened to you?"

Before Bruce could answer, he collapsed to the ground.

# CHAPTER
# FORTY-SIX

"UNTIL WE KNOW what's going on here, I want the two of you to stay in town." Liberman shifted in front of Hayes and Addie as they stood outside.

A half hour had passed since Bruce emerged from the woods.

Everyone still lingered near the ambulance, and law enforcement vehicles surrounded them, casting their blue and red lights into the night.

The temperature had dropped even more, leaving a biting chill in the air.

But Liberman's words sent a different kind of chill through Hayes.

His chest tightened. The last thing he wanted to do was to stay here. Not when trouble was so close.

What he wanted was to whisk Addie away to somewhere safe.

He rubbed his jaw as he turned toward the sheriff. "Is that really necessary?"

"Until I know the extent of what's happening, you need to stay in the area." Liberman gave him a pointed look.

Hayes knew what that meant. Liberman considered Hayes and Addie suspects. They were the ones in closest proximity to Bruce and Brianna. There was a rift between them. And Hayes and Addie had found that burned corpse, which had later disappeared.

But he didn't like the sound of any of this.

The only comfort Hayes had was in knowing his colleagues at Vanishing Ranch were on their way. They probably wouldn't arrive until morning, but at least he'd have some backup.

"What about Bruce?" Hayes glanced at the man as paramedics treated him in the ambulance.

"He's lost a lot of blood. I don't know how long it will be before I can ask him any questions. If ever."

That much was clear.

He only wished the man could speak now. That he could tell them what was going on. Where Brianna was.

Hayes remembered the update he'd gotten from his friend earlier. He needed to let the sheriff know about it. "By the way, Bruce has a past. He's been arrested on drug charges before."

The sheriff narrowed his eyes. "Been doing your own research?"

"Hazard of the job, I suppose."

The sheriff grunted. "I guess so."

"And what about Brianna?" Addie stepped closer, worry staining her voice. "Are you sending guys out to search for her? What if she's hurt?"

"I already sent two of my deputies to look for her. But it's not safe to be out in these woods at night, as the two of you well know." Liberman nodded at Hayes's leg, reminding them about the bear trap. "I told my guys to come back in an hour if they don't find anything."

"But she could be hurt." Addie's voice cracked.

"We're well aware of that." Liberman's jaw hardened with determination and maybe a touch of weariness. "We're doing everything within our power to locate her. Unfortunately, it's going to take some time. The wilderness around us is nothing to play with."

Neither of them argued with his words.

Just then, Deputy Clark came running from the woods.

Hayes braced himself for more bad news.

"Sheriff . . . we found a car. And someone is inside it. She's dead."

Hayes's heart rate quickened.

"Where is it?" Liberman asked as he stepped toward the woods.

"It's off a service road about a half mile away. The car was in bad condition—rusty with plastic over one of the windows."

Hayes and Addie exchanged a glance.

It was the car the general store clerk had mentioned seeing Bruce in, wasn't it?

"What about the body inside?" Liberman asked. "Did you recognize her?"

"No, sir."

Liberman muttered something beneath his breath before saying, "We're going to need to get out there. Backup has been delayed due to some big SWAT incident to the west of us."

Paramedics closed the ambulance doors and began to head to the nearest hospital, leaving only Liberman, Deputy Clark, Hayes, and Addie standing there.

Liberman didn't look happy as he stared at the woods, no doubt trying to figure out his next move.

Before he could speak, shuffling sounded in the woods.

Then a shot rang out.

Hayes threw Addie onto the ground and lay on top of her.

Then more gunfire blasted through the air.

Liberman and Clark had been hit. They were on the ground and out of commission.

That meant Hayes and Addie were on their own . . . and there was definitely more than one gunman surrounding this place.

———

"We've got to move!" Hayes shouted. "Come on!"

"What about Liberman and Clark?" Addie remained frozen with fear.

"We'll be no good to them dead. Hopefully, the SWAT team can wrap up their incident and be here soon. I'm praying they get here in time."

Before Addie could ask more questions, he grabbed her hand. "Stay low!"

He pulled her toward their cabin—toward safety. At least, it would provide some temporary safety, Addie mused.

Gunshots flew around them, splintering the wood of the cabin and deck.

They had to keep moving. Staying still, they'd be too easy as targets.

Hayes continued pulling Addie until they

climbed the deck and reached the back door. He threw it open, pushed her inside, then locked the door behind him.

He led Addie into a hallway, away from any windows, and pulled out his gun.

She was surprised he hadn't pulled it out earlier, but it probably wouldn't have done much good. They were too outnumbered.

Addie wasn't sure how many guys were out there, but she'd guess at least three.

When Addie glanced around the corner, she didn't see anyone outside the cabin.

Not yet.

"What's happening?" Addie muttered as she glanced back up at Hayes.

He pulled her back again. "I don't know. Let's just wait this out and see what happens."

"What if Bruce set us up?" Her voice cracked under the strain of the situation. "What if whoever attacked Bruce is after us too? Maybe they think we're involved."

"I don't know what's going on with Bruce, and I don't think he's been truthful. But he truly was hurt, so whatever was going on, he's in bad shape because of it."

Addie glanced at her phone, hoping that she might have cell service again.

But she didn't.

Frowning, she slipped her phone back in her pocket and waited.

She didn't know how this was going to turn out, but danger hung in the air.

What were those guys doing out there? Were they moving in on them? How was the sheriff? Deputy Clark? Had they even survived?

And what she wanted to know even more: how long would it be before backup arrived?

# CHAPTER
# FORTY-SEVEN

HAYES TRIED to hide his worry, but he wasn't succeeding.

Bruce had clearly found himself involved in some type of trouble—trouble that had followed him back here to the cabin. The Guardian could also be here. He didn't think the two were one and the same.

For now, Hayes tried to bide his time until backup arrived.

He watched the windows, certain the shooters would approach the cabin. He could hold them off for a while. But he was clearly outnumbered.

"It's going to be okay," he murmured.

He wrapped an arm around Addie, wishing he could comfort her more.

But he couldn't.

Not right now.

One look at her face, and he knew she was blaming this on herself. She'd been the one who'd come here. Who'd interfered with Bruce and Brianna.

How could he convince her that this wasn't her fault?

Was it even possible?

"Addie . . ." Hayes pushed her hair away from her face as he looked down at her.

Her gaze seemed to hesitantly meet his. "This was all a bad idea, wasn't it? I never wanted you to be put in this position."

"We're in this together. That's how marriage works."

"And I feel like my trouble has attached itself to you. I don't want to ruin your life."

He heard the truth in her words. Heard the echoes of the words Addie's mom used to say to her. Those words made up her inner critic now.

Before he could comment, the door burst open.

Hayes's back stiffened as he gripped his gun and shoved Addie behind him.

———

Fear raced through Addie as three men with guns flooded the space.

"Put it down," one of the masked men said. "Or we'll shoot. No questions asked."

"Don't do anything drastic," Hayes muttered as he placed his gun on the floor and slid it to them.

"Now, step over here," the same man said.

They did as he said.

Addie's heart pounded harder as she stared at the men.

They were wearing masks, but . . . they didn't look or sound familiar.

Who were these guys?

Hayes raised his hands as he clearly realized he was outnumbered. "We don't want any trouble."

"Where are they?" The man in the middle stepped forward. This guy was taller than the others —and broader too. He had a slight accent, though Addie couldn't place it.

"What do you mean?" Hayes moved himself farther in front of Addie.

"You know what I'm talking about. Give us what's rightfully ours or she'll die." He pointed his gun at Addie.

Another shiver of fear raced through her.

"I'm telling you, I don't know what you're talking about." Hayes appeared tense and on guard—more than she'd ever seen him before.

"He said he gave them to you."

"Who gave what to me?" A knot formed between Hayes's eyes.

Even as Hayes asked the question, Addie thought she knew the answer.

It was Bruce, wasn't it? He'd taken something from these guys and decided Hayes and Addie would be the perfect scapegoats.

"The stolen drugs," the man growled. "That guy said he gave them to you. So where are they?"

Addie's thoughts raced.

She didn't know anything about any drugs.

But she had a feeling these guys weren't going to believe anything she or Hayes said.

She swallowed hard and dreaded what they might have to endure as they tried to convince these men of the truth.

HAYES'S THOUGHTS RACED. "We don't have any drugs. I don't know who told you that, but we're not involved."

"I beg to differ." The man's demanding voice held no patience for reasoning. "Someone stole the drugs, and now my dealer is looking for them. If I don't get them back, then I'm gonna die. But you're gonna die before I do. So you might as well start talking."

Hayes quickly thought through the situation. He remembered Bruce getting on that boat. Remembered seeing that map left out in his cabin. Remembered Bruce talking about that small island that was his magical fishing spot.

His thoughts continued to race.

Had Bruce stolen drugs from these guys and hidden them on that island?

Was that what was going on? Were Bruce and Brianna trying to escape tonight before these guys caught them?

Hayes had no idea, but that was his best guess right now.

"I'm getting tired of this silence!" The ringleader pulled the trigger and fired into the ceiling.

As pieces of wood rained down around them, Addie let out a muffled scream and ducked.

The situation was quickly escalating.

Hayes stepped forward, knowing he had to do something. "Listen, I didn't take your drugs, but I think I know where Bruce may have put them."

The man's eyes narrowed. "Where?"

"On an island out in the lake."

"Is that right?" The man's tone almost sounded mocking. "Show us."

"Only if you let her go." Hayes nodded toward Addie.

"It's not gonna be that easy." He motioned to one of the other men, and the guy grabbed Addie and placed a gun to her head. "In fact, why don't I make this simple for you? You take us to those drugs or she's going to die. Right here. Right now."

Addie's heart raced as the threat hung in the air.

"I'll do it." Hayes's voice sounded even but cautious.

"No!" The word flew from Addie's lips, almost sounding like a guttural cry. "Don't do it."

If Hayes took them out there, they were going to kill him whether or not he found what they were looking for. That was how this would all end.

Addie felt certain of it.

"Shut up!" The man beside her smacked his gun across her jaw.

Pain raced through her as she grasped the area.

She looked up and saw Hayes had bristled. His hands were fisted and his face red.

But these guys had guns, and he didn't. They were too outnumbered to do anything except comply.

"If you don't start talking, there's more of that where it came from," the man muttered.

"I said I would take you to find them," Hayes said through gritted teeth. "But not if you hurt her."

"I don't think you're in a good position to be calling the shots right now," the ringleader said.

Hayes scowled. "Do you want to know where the drugs are or not?"

"We do. And we want you to take us there."

The man pressed the gun into Addie's temple again until she let out a cry.

Hayes was probably hoping this would buy some time. That backup would arrive soon.

Did these guys know more officers were headed this way?

Addie hoped not. That information could be just the wild card they needed.

Right now, Hayes was going to try to appease the men in this situation by trying to find the drugs.

Addie hoped he was right when he said he knew where Bruce had gone.

Otherwise . . . they were both dead.

ADDIE'S HEART felt like it was breaking as she watched two gunmen walk away with Hayes.

What kind of situation had they gotten themselves into?

For sure, this wouldn't end well.

They'd left her alone with the man who had smacked her in the jaw. He pulled his mask off, revealing he was thirty-something with pale skin and blond hair. He sucked in several deep breaths as if he hadn't been able to breathe.

But the fact he was showing his face wasn't a good sign.

It most likely meant she wouldn't make it out of here alive.

She glowered at him as they stood there. "Why are you doing this?"

He narrowed his eyes as he glared back at her. "You took something that belongs to us."

"I didn't take anything!"

He grunted as if he didn't believe her.

"Are you the one who's been behind these vandalisms in the area?" Addie asked, her thoughts racing. "Did you hit Hayes over the head?"

"We tried to warn him to leave. He didn't get the hint."

"And so you left the message painted on our cabin."

"These rentals weren't supposed to be occupied. We were banking on that. That's why we chose this area as our headquarters. We couldn't have anyone messing up our plans."

"Are you the one who pushed me off the cliff also?"

He squinted. "What? No. Why would I do that?"

Her throat tightened. That's what she'd thought.

There was more than one kind of danger going on here.

The Guardian was also nearby.

She couldn't think about that right now. She had to keep her thoughts focused. The more information she could find out, the more easily she could form a plan.

She needed to find a way out of this and help Hayes before it was too late.

Addie licked her lips before asking, "If these drugs are so valuable, why did you leave them somewhere they could easily be stolen?"

He practically growled at her before saying, "We sent them to a designated drop site. But that guy grabbed them before the buyers could. Now my dealer is out a lot of money, and somebody's going to pay."

"How much money are you talking about?"

"Enough to kill for." Vengeance rang from the man's tone.

These guys were out for blood.

Hayes and Addie were in the crossfire.

Addie crossed her arms over her chest and shivered.

She only prayed that Hayes would make it out of this alive.

————

Each of Hayes's muscles were rigid as he led the men through the woods.

He'd glanced at Liberman and Clark as he passed. They were alive, but he didn't know for how much longer that would be true.

He knew one other deputy was still out here—the one who was with Clark when they found the abandoned car with the body inside.

Hayes only assumed the deputy remained with the vehicle to guard the body and preserve evidence.

Whoever that was who'd been killed . . . these guys had done it, hadn't they?

Then they'd nearly killed Bruce.

They weren't afraid to take people's lives. That was clear.

He prayed that Addie would be safe. That the man left with her wouldn't do anything to harm her.

She'd survived so much trauma already. Had been through so much.

But Hayes knew this was far from being over.

Even if he and Addie managed to outsmart these guys . . . the men with him now weren't the ones who'd been sending those threatening texts to Addie. He suspected they weren't the ones who'd pushed her over that cliff either.

Danger was coming at them from all sides, and it would take every bit of his law enforcement training to come out on the other side.

"We know who you are," the man behind Hayes said.

"Who am I?" Hayes's throat tightened as he waited for the man's response.

"You used to be with Homeland Security. We do our research."

Hayes had to at least give them credit for that.

"I'm not sure how you think that fact is going to help you find these drugs," Hayes muttered.

"It means you're smart enough to know we mean business," the leader barked. "I need those drugs. I needed them yesterday, for that matter."

"I get it. There are bills to pay."

"And reputations to uphold. A man's word means everything."

Hayes couldn't argue with that. He'd promised to love Addie for life. And he had every intention of honoring that promise.

Which meant he had to find a way to survive this and get back to her before anything bad happened.

His thoughts raced as they continued through the dark woods.

"Did you leave that bear trap?" Hayes tried to put more pieces together.

"We thought it might be a nice deterrent." Humor laced the man's voice.

"And the body I saw near the lake. Was that your work too?"

The man chuckled. "That's right. We figured that Bruce guy and his wife were involved. That they were working with that other couple. We had to teach them a lesson, to show them what happens to people who think they can steal from us."

So Brianna *had* run into a friend while she was in town. Together, the group must have stumbled across the drugs somewhere and realized they'd hit the jackpot. That had to be the case if these guys were taking things to this extreme. It had to be a lot of drugs that had gone missing.

If his theory was correct, someone in that group had found the drugs and then Bruce had hidden them on the island. It was a good place to stash them —somewhere no one would find them. The cabin or one of their vehicles would be too obvious.

Bruce had probably launched his boat from this area either because it was closer to the island or to avoid being seen.

But after Bruce and his friend got back from the island, these guys must have found his friend and killed him.

When Bruce had been talking about "getting rid of it," they weren't talking about Brianna's body. Maybe they were talking about the drugs. Maybe they realized they were in too deep.

Hayes was halfway surprised Bruce hadn't realized how dangerous this was, considering he'd been convicted of drug charges before. But maybe his desire for a quick payout had beat his desire for safety.

As they walked through the woods, Hayes heard the two men with him talking.

The ringleader's name was Ralph. They'd come down from Canada, apparently.

This was an international drug ring, Hayes realized. That meant the stakes were even higher. More money was involved. More people.

They were almost at the boat ramp. As they got closer, Hayes spotted another bear trap in the brush. He'd been looking for them, especially after his last scare. He carefully walked around it, trying not to alert anyone it was there.

It could work in his favor later.

Hayes stopped at the area where he'd seen Bruce get into the boat with that other guy.

A rowboat had been left there.

"You have to take that to get to the island," Hayes said. "That's where Bruce stashed the drugs for safekeeping. No one goes there at this time of year. It's too cold. Too dangerous—especially with the snow this week."

"You're going to go get it for us," Ralph growled.

Hayes's eyebrows shot up. "You want me to paddle out there by myself?"

"That's right. You go out there, you get it, you

bring it back. If you don't, your wife is going to die. Do you understand?"

Hayes had no doubt he was telling the truth. The best thing he could do right now was to comply. "Understood."

ADDIE STARED at the gunman as he shifted beside her.

He was impatient, wasn't he? He didn't want to be here with her, but he'd apparently drawn the short straw.

Still, she'd seen what these guys had done to law enforcement outside. She knew they weren't to be played with.

As she stood there, her thoughts drifted to the upcoming holidays.

Specifically to Thanksgiving, which was only a week away.

She'd always loved celebrating with Hayes and his family.

This year she'd resigned herself just to eat alone or maybe—*maybe*—have a couple people from the studio over to eat with her. But now Danielle was missing, and no one had heard from Geraldo and Julia.

She didn't feel like celebrating—not after all that had happened. Especially if her friends were hurt or . . . worse.

In truth, she'd been dreading the holiday this year.

Especially since her two-year anniversary with Hayes preceded it.

Their wedding had truly been one of the happiest days of her life. They'd kept it simple and lowkey.

Addie had bought a white sundress, and Hayes had worn khakis and a white shirt. They'd gone to the beach at sunset, and their pastor had married them in the presence of a handful of family and friends.

The ceremony had been perfect.

Tears pressed at her eyes.

She couldn't just stand here and mentally replay the best moments of her life as if she were going to die.

Hayes was out there in trouble.

He needed her.

Addie glanced at the gunman as he shifted beside her. He pulled out his phone and began to play a game, clearly bored.

This man who was keeping guard of her evidently thought she was helpless and not much of a threat.

Her mind raced.

She needed to use that to her advantage.

———

The icy cold water of the lake moistened the edges of Hayes's jeans and sent shivers through him.

It wasn't the time of the year he wanted to be out on this lake—especially not at night when it was hard to see. Where the boat could easily run into a large rock hidden just beneath the surface.

But he didn't have much of a choice right now.

With Ralph's gun still pointed at him, Hayes climbed aboard the small rowboat and began to paddle. He hoped to remember where the island was and how to get there from the map he'd seen. At least, the moonlight would help guide his way.

But what if the drugs weren't there when he arrived? What would he do then? This was all just a guess.

Hayes knew exactly what these guys would do if he came back empty-handed.

They would kill Addie.

His gut clenched at the thought of it.

He rowed, and rowed, and rowed. Finally, he spotted the island Bruce had told him about.

The magical fishing spot as Bruce had called it.

It wasn't big. Maybe twenty feet in diameter and mostly made up of rocks. But several trees had grown on the stony surface.

Hayes circled halfway around the island before finding a place to pull ashore.

Whatever he did, he couldn't lose track of this boat. If so, he'd be stuck on this island, and no one would know where he was. Swimming back to shore wasn't an option. Hypothermia would get him first.

Carefully, he climbed out and pulled the boat onto the rocky shore, making sure it was secure.

Then he glanced around the small patch of land, hoping he could find the drugs these guys were looking for.

But before he could move, a noise sounded.

He froze.

He wasn't alone on this island, was he?

# CHAPTER
# FIFTY-ONE

BEFORE ADDIE LOST HER COURAGE, she pointed at the man, and her eyes widened.

"Your face . . ."

"What about it?" The man's voice rose with alarm.

"You've got a rash all over it. It's all splotchy and turning red."

"A rash?" The man glanced in a mirror beside him.

As he did, Addie grabbed the lamp beside her and swung it with all her might.

The wooden base hit his head.

The man dropped to the floor.

Her heart pounded hard as she stared at him.

She'd done it.

He was out cold.

Part of her didn't believe it.

She didn't have time to stand here and question herself, however.

Quickly, she grabbed his gun. She prayed she wouldn't have to use it.

Then she ran outside.

As she passed Deputy Clark and Sheriff Liberman, she paused.

"Are you two good?" She knelt beside the sheriff.

He moaned and grasped his shoulder. "I'm . . . okay . . . go . . . get them."

She stared at him one more minute before nodding. "Backup should be here soon, right? The SWAT guys?"

He blinked and barely nodded.

She took the scarf from around her neck and pressed it into his wound. "Can you hold this there?"

He muttered something, and his hand covered the scarf. At least it was something.

She used her knit hat to put pressure on Clark's abdominal wound.

Then she stood and frowned.

She didn't want to leave them.

But right now, she had no choice.

There was little she could do to help, and time was of the essence.

Instead, she glanced around, noticing just how quiet and still it was.

Had Hayes reached the island yet?

She ran to the edge of the water and looked out.

As she glanced around, a light on the other side of the lake caught her eye.

Someone was over there.

But who? Could it be Hayes?

Possibly.

But it could also be the dealer who was coming to hunt these guys down and find the drugs that had been stolen from him.

Addie couldn't just stand here.

She had to do something.

With that thought, she charged into the woods.

———

Hayes froze as he listened to the sound. As he anticipated what would happen.

The next instant, a huge bird fluttered through the trees, squawking as it took flight.

Hayes had obviously disturbed it.

He let out the breath he held.

It was just a bird, not a rival drug runner looking for the missing stash.

That should make this all a little easier.

He scolded himself. He was really on edge. But how could he not be, considering everything that had happened?

He began searching the island.

After walking around the entire place three times, Hayes had found nothing.

He paused near his boat and tried to pivot his thoughts.

If the drugs weren't here, then where would they be?

He turned and glanced back at the rocky patch of land. Sure, there were nooks and crannies here where drugs could have been hidden. He'd tried to search them all with his flashlight.

He hadn't found anything.

Now he was running out of time.

So where would Bruce have put the drugs?

Certainly, he wouldn't have stashed them at the cabin. Would he?

Hayes was out of ideas.

He sighed and glanced up, lifting a quick prayer for wisdom.

That's when he saw it.

A black plastic bag had been strung in a tree. The moonlight hit it, illuminating it for a moment.

Hunters and campers did that sometimes to keep

their food off the ground, so no unexpected visitors came at night.

Here, the bag blended in with the shadows, making it nearly impossible to see—except for that moonlight.

He'd almost missed it. He thanked God he hadn't.

After using a knife to cut the rope, the bag dropped to the ground.

Hayes then used his knife to slice open a small section of plastic.

Packages of white powder were stored inside.

Heroin.

The drugs these guys were looking for.

Hayes tucked the bag under his arm and scrambled back down the rocks to the boat.

He didn't know how things would play out once he met these guys again.

But at least he had some leverage now.

Quickly, he climbed in the boat and paddled back across the water.

The guys waited for him on the shore looking anxious. They'd taken off their masks, revealing blond hair and pale features.

Seeing their faces was a bad sign.

He knew they weren't going to let him walk away from this.

They waited until Hayes had pushed the boat ashore before they spoke.

"Well?" Ralph paced closer, gun still in hand.

Hayes stood, climbing out of the boat. Then he grabbed the bag and held it up. "I found it. Now you need to let Addie go."

"First, let me see what's in that bag."

He tossed it toward them.

The guy caught it and pulled open the small cut Hayes had made.

Hayes held his breath as he waited to see what the man would do next.

But a moment later, Ralph dipped his finger into the powder and placed it in his mouth.

A smile spread across his face. "Well done."

Now, these guys had what they wanted.

Hayes knew what that meant.

Ralph raised his gun at Hayes.

About to shoot.

Hayes braced himself.

"Sorry it has to end this way," Ralph muttered.

But before he could pull the trigger, someone lunged from the shadows and tackled Ralph.

ADDIE KNEW what she was doing was risky. That it could get her killed.

But she had no other choice.

She had to help Hayes.

She remembered that boat ride Bruce had taken. Where he'd left from shore that time.

That's when she realized the light that she'd seen was coming from that same area he'd rowed toward.

Quietly, she'd moved through the woods until she found these guys.

She heard them talking.

Knew they planned on killing both her and Hayes as soon as they got what they wanted.

She couldn't let that happen.

For now, she waited.

When she heard water splashing, she moved in closer.

A moment later, a boat appeared.

Her heartbeat quickened.

It was Hayes.

She listened as he came ashore and tossed something to those men.

He'd managed to find the drugs.

Relief and trepidation swept through her at the same time.

But her relief was short-lived.

As soon as that one guy raised his gun to Hayes, she knew she had to act.

Even though she had a gun, she wasn't planning to shoot the guy in the back. She'd use it only if she had to.

She needed to at least buy them some time.

Using her kickboxing moves, she darted from the woods. She swung her leg and knocked the ringleader off his feet. His gun flew through the air.

The man landed on his back. As soon as he did, the man grabbed her leg and jerked her to the ground.

On top of him.

"What do you think you're doing?" the man muttered beneath her.

She tried to elbow his throat. But he was too strong.

With one move, he threw her off of him and onto the ground.

Addie's back hit a rock, and a moan escaped from her as pain shot through her.

But somehow, Addie kept her thoughts clear enough to reach the gun and toss it toward Hayes. "Here!"

He caught it and pointed it at the other guy—who also had his gun drawn.

Addie pulled herself up and leaned back on the palms of her hands. More pain rushed through her, but she ignored it.

For now.

"This isn't going to end well," the ringleader said as he sneered at Hayes, blood rushing from his nose.

"We all have what we want." Hayes remained calm and in control. "So why don't you just walk away?"

"I can't do that." The man dragged himself to his feet and scowled as he wiped his nose and saw the red there. "You've seen our faces."

"We have."

"Don't tell me you won't report us," the man said. "You were Homeland Security. Of course, you will."

"Maybe I will." Hayes still held his gun. "But at least you'll have a running head start."

"Let's face it. You're outnumbered. Just put the gun down."

"No," Hayes said.

Addie crawled away from them, moving closer to Hayes.

"I'm done with this!" the ringleader said. "Shoot him!"

But before his henchman could pull the trigger, gunfire rang out again.

Two shots, actually.

The ringleader fell to the ground, immediately followed by his henchman.

But when Addie looked at Hayes, she realized he wasn't the one who'd fired.

---

Hayes glanced over as a shadow emerged from the darkness.

It was him.

The man who'd been going after Addie.

Who'd made her life a living nightmare over the past several months.

The man who referred to himself as The Guardian.

"You can thank me later," the man muttered.

The shooter's face came into view.

Hayes realized he didn't recognize the man with dark, thick hair and a brawny build.

This guy wasn't someone he'd put in prison.

But something about him and his craggy features looked vaguely familiar. What was it?

Addie gasped beside him. "Ethan?"

Ethan? Who was Ethan?

The man offered a crooked smile. "The one and only."

"Ethan . . ." Addie's voice trembled. "It's been you this whole time? What did I ever do to you? Why have you been tormenting me?"

"Because I promised my brother that I would make sure you were never happy again."

Hayes's breath caught. Ethan . . . this was Reggie's brother, wasn't it? They shared some of the same traits.

But he was in prison.

When had he gotten out? And why hadn't anyone let Addie know?

"What?" Addie sounded breathless. "Why would you promise him that?"

He sneered and stepped closer. "Reggie never got over losing you. I couldn't stand to see him suffer and not do anything about it."

"But he's been dead nearly three years. Why do this now?"

He shrugged. "I was in prison. I had to wait until I was out. First, I took care of Amy. After all, Reggie said it was all her fault you left him. Then I had to make sure you and this guy were never together again. I could have killed him, I guess, but that would have been too easy."

Hayes stepped forward, worried about the gun in the man's hand. He had his own weapon, but there was too much at stake here to simply pull the trigger and hope for the best. Ethan could easily turn his gun on Addie.

"You don't have to do this," Hayes muttered.

Ethan smirked. "Of course, I do. Reggie and I made a pact when we were kids. We always kept our promises to each other." His gaze darkened as he looked back at Addie. "You made a promise to him too. And you broke your promise."

"Only because he hurt me." Trembles overtook Addie. "You know he did."

"Only because you deserved it. I need to make things right now." Ethan aimed his gun at Hayes.

Hayes knew he had to think quickly, or he was going to die.

———

As soon as Addie saw the gun pointed at Hayes, panic raced through her.

She hadn't come this far for things to end like this.

Yet she knew Ethan was entirely capable of pulling the trigger—all as revenge for his brother. They'd always had a close bond, but she'd never suspected this.

"It's okay," Hayes muttered as he stepped forward. "I know I'm the one you want out of the picture. Take me. Just don't kill me in front of Addie. Reggie wouldn't want that."

"How would you know what Reggie would want?" Ethan spit out the words.

"Your brother was misunderstood." Hayes took another step closer.

What was he doing? Addie wondered. Was he really taking Reggie's side?

Then she realized the truth.

Hayes was bluffing.

Buying time.

Formulating a plan.

"That's right," Ethan barked. "Reggie was misunderstood. By everyone. He deserved better."

"And so do you," Hayes muttered. "You were dealt a bad hand as well."

"Reggie and I both were. It wasn't supposed to be this way. It's not fair."

Addie held her breath as she waited for Hayes's next move.

"When you love someone, you'll do whatever it takes to protect them," Hayes muttered. "Am I right?"

"Absolutely."

"No matter the cost."

The next instant, he charged at Ethan.

Caught him in his midsection.

Threw him to the ground.

A snap sounded.

The gun discharged and flew from Ethan's hand as he howled with pain and reached for his abdomen.

A bear trap, Addie realized.

He'd fallen into a bear trap.

Addie held her breath as she waited for whatever would happen next.

But she was sure that when Hayes had said you do whatever you have to do to protect those you love at any cost, he was talking about her.

ETHAN WAS STRONGER than Hayes had anticipated.

But that wasn't going to slow him down.

If Hayes failed now, both he and Addie would die.

He couldn't let that happen.

Despite the bear trap, Ethan tried to rise up. He must be operating on pure adrenaline and energy.

As he did, Hayes swung his fist and hit him in the jaw.

Ethan moaned and sank back to the ground.

With one more punch to the face, the man crumpled, totally blacked out.

Hayes rose and sucked in a deep breath.

Then he glanced at Addie.

She looked ashen and shaky.

But otherwise, she was okay.

She ran toward him, and he enveloped her with his arms.

"I'm so glad you're okay," he murmured.

"I can't believe this might be over."

Two drug runners and one psycho former inmate lay on the ground injured and moaning around them.

The odds hadn't been in their favor.

But they'd overcome them.

He hoped that would be the case for their marriage as well.

Just then, footsteps pounded through the woods.

Were the head drug dealer and his men coming now?

The way things were going, Hayes wouldn't be surprised.

Hayes gripped the gun in his hand.

Instead, sheriff's deputies surrounded them. As they took over the scene, Hayes finally felt his shoulders ease some.

Maybe this was truly all over.

———

Three hours later, Addie and Hayes were back at the cabin.

She had a blanket wrapped around her shoulders

and a cup of coffee in hand as law enforcement milled around. Three of Hayes's colleagues from Vanishing Ranch had also shown up to help.

One of the deputies from a neighboring county had taken their statements and made numerous arrests. Apparently, the other incident that had held the SWAT team up involved this drug lord who wanted the heroin. He was now in jail.

Sheriff Liberman and Deputy Clark had been taken to the hospital. They were both in critical condition but were in good hands now.

The body from the car in the woods had been retrieved. The vehicle had belonged to Rick and Lisa Wilson from Nevada. It appeared they were friends with Bruce and Brianna. Rick had been killed first and his body left on the shore. Lisa's body had been found in the car.

All of this pain . . . all because of some drugs. It was a shame.

Speaking of Brianna . . . Addie glanced around. Where was she?

Those men hadn't mentioned killing her. But . . .

As someone else stepped inside, her breath caught.

Brianna.

Addie rushed toward her, so glad she was okay.

She appeared uninjured as she paused in front of Addie.

"You're alive," Addie murmured. "I thought something had happened. Where have you been?"

Brianna frowned and shivered. "I'm okay. I was hiding at one of the empty cabins up the road. It was cold. But I saw what those men did to Bruce and . . . I ran. I didn't know what else to do. I thought they were going to kill me also."

"Brianna . . . has Bruce been hurting you? We saw the drops of blood on your countertop. I saw your bruises."

Brianna shrugged and shook her head. "I cut myself while making dinner. And then . . . our friends called and asked us to meet them right away. We decided to finish cooking later. And the bruises . . . well, I really am clumsy. As far as Bruce and me . . . I mean, we get heated. We drive each other crazy. But he's never laid a hand on me."

"I'm glad to hear that. Because if he does—"

"He won't." Brianna's chin trembled, but her eyes held steady.

Addie studied Brianna's face a moment before realizing she was telling the truth. Addie had sensed a volatile situation, but it was because of the stolen drugs, not abuse.

"What happened?" Hayes stepped closer. "Why did those guys come after you?"

Brianna wiped beneath her eyes. "Bruce and I were out for a walk, and we found a man in the water. He was dead, and he had a backpack on him. We were trying to find his ID. We found drugs instead."

They waited for her to continue. She sucked in several deep breaths.

"We didn't know what to do. We found out later, when those men found us in the woods, that this guy was supposed to deliver the drugs, but he must have slipped off one of the rocks and into the lake. Anyway, we knew the drugs were worth a lot—and that we could use them to our advantage. But we didn't want to bring them back to our cabin. It seemed too dangerous. So Bruce hid them on the island. But those guys figured out what we'd done and started to hunt us."

"So you set us up to take the fall in the meantime?" Hayes stared at her as he waited for her reaction.

She frowned and wiped more tears away. "We didn't mean to. But you kept asking questions. It was Bruce's idea. We thought we could throw them off our scent and get out of town. But we weren't able to get back out to the island and retrieve them. Too many people were watching."

Addie shook her head. "So you two were just going to sneak off into the night and leave us to deal with the consequences."

"I . . . I'm sorry."

One of the deputies came and led Brianna away. No doubt, she'd be facing multiple charges.

"Good news," Hayes said softly. "I just heard from Mateo that they found Danielle. She'd been tied up and left at Ethan's house. She's shaken but okay."

Relief washed through her. "That's wonderful news. What about my friends who own the cabin? Geraldo and Julia?"

"They're also okay. Ethan was just trying to get information out of them about where you were. Apparently, it worked."

"I'm so glad they're okay. That everyone is okay."

Hayes wrapped his arms around Addie, and she curled into him.

"I'm so sorry," she murmured into his chest.

"No more apologizing," he whispered. "I'm sorry you were in this situation."

"I didn't know what to do. I only wanted you to be safe—"

"I know," he said softly.

Addie pulled back slightly. She needed to see his eyes. "You do?"

"I do. You always try to look out for others. I'm just glad this is all over. No more secrets?"

"No more secrets." She reached up on her tiptoes and planted a kiss on his lips.

Maybe all things truly had worked out for the best, despite the crazy path to get here.

HAYES GLANCED into the dining hall at Vanishing Ranch and smiled.

He had planned to spend Thanksgiving with his family, but his parents had decided to go visit his brother in Costa Rica instead.

That's when he'd asked Addie if she might be interested in coming to Vanishing Ranch with him.

She'd jumped at the prospect. Helping other women who'd been in similar situations as hers was one of her passions.

The smell of turkey, gravy, and mashed potatoes filled the air. Upbeat music softly played in the room. There were probably sixteen guests—women whom the staff here were helping. Then there were the ten or so staff members who'd stayed for the holiday as well.

Everyone had pitched in to help with the dinner.

Some of the women had decorated the table with burlap and candles and some paper turkeys, made by a couple of the children staying here.

Chef had spent all day making some of his specialties. But a few other people had pitched in to contribute their favorite dishes also.

Charlie Soldier, who ran the ranch, had made her famous brussels sprouts, pecan, and cranberry salad. The dish didn't sound appealing to him, but everyone raved about how good it was.

Amberly, Charlie's daughter who'd recently reappeared in Charlie's life, stood on the other side of the room talking to one of the ranch hands. She wasn't quite fitting in here, and she had a rebellious glint in her gaze.

But she hadn't been here long. She just needed more time.

He glanced at the crowd around him. Newlyweds Jesse and Sienna. Pilot Ghost and movie star Chesney. Ruger and Sarah. Mateo and Emily. Carter and new recruit Ainsley.

Hayes had no doubt that one day, these people would all feel like family to him also.

Addie wrapped her arms around his waist as they stood beside each other, staring at the scene.

"I like it here," she said. "I can see why you took this job."

"It's a pretty great place with a pretty great mission."

"Absolutely."

The past week since they'd left Lake Tahoe had been fantastic.

They still weren't exactly where they needed to be, but they'd come so far. They would both go to counseling together so they could work through some of the issues that stood between them. Considering everything that had happened in Addie's past, she had things in her life that she needed to work through. And Hayes needed to figure out how to work through them with her.

But one thing was for sure. Having open, honest communication was essential.

Still, Hayes was thankful they were working through things and back together.

He knew that when Addie had lost her brother when she was younger, it had been difficult, to say the least. That guilt, which was compounded by her mother, combined with what happened with Reggie had created some major obstacles. Obstacles that could be overcome. But it would take time and prayer.

But he remembered the verse that they'd just had

a friend print for them. They'd framed it and had hung it on their wall back at their place in San Diego.

*And we know that in all things God works for the good of those who love him, who've been called according to his purpose.*

Hayes believed that as well.

Everyone's attention seemed to drift toward the door.

He turned to see what the commotion was about.

A grin stretched across his face when he saw Hudson and Teagan enter the dining hall with their new little baby boy.

Everyone began to ooh and aah over him.

Hayes smiled.

He was happy for his new friend. Hudson and his wife truly looked like they were on top of the world right now.

"I hope one day that can be us," Addie murmured.

His heart skipped a beat. "You think you're ready for kids?"

"Not yet. But I'm hoping I will be soon. Because I want to have babies. With you. I want the American dream. I know it's going to come with a lot of hard work. I know I have things to overcome. But you're right. I can do this. Especially if you're with me."

He leaned closer and planted a long kiss on her

lips. "I'll always be at your side. And I'll always have your back. Never doubt that. Okay?"

More tears of joy flooded her eyes. "I'll never doubt that. You've proven it to me time and time again." She opened her mouth, and he knew she was about to apologize again.

But she stopped herself and smiled instead.

"It's been quite a journey, hasn't it?"

"It sure has. But there's no one else I'd rather do it with than you. We truly do have so much to be thankful for."

Hayes grinned. "Yes, we do."

~~~

Thank you for reading *Fatal Vendetta*. If you enjoyed this book, please consider leaving a review.

Keep reading for a preview of *Troubled Tidings*!
~~~

USA TODAY BESTSELLING AUTHOR
CHRISTY BARRITT
Troubled
TIDINGS
VANISHING RANCH
THE SERIES - BOOK EIGHT

# TROUBLED TIDINGS: CHAPTER ONE

"Eighteen-year-old Jacob Carlson has been missing for ten days now." A female newscaster's voice floated through the speaker on Dean Burns's phone. "He went for a hike in the Mojave Desert and hasn't been seen since."

Didn't people know they should never hike alone? Dean shook his head as he traveled down the lonely road in his truck. He hoped someone found the missing guy. What a terrible ordeal his family must be going through.

"Also, beware of the Roadside Bandits who have been hitting the area for the past two months," the newscaster continued. "It's been a few days since they were known to be active, which means they're due to strike again. Who would do this at Christmas-time, you might be wondering? That's what we'd all like to know also. Anyone with information, please contact . . ."

"How can you even listen to that?" Kota Perez glanced over at him from the passenger seat.

He shrugged. "What can I say? I guess I like to stay informed, Miss Kota."

"How about staying informed about good things instead?"

"That's a great suggestion. I'll take it under consideration."

She raised her eyebrows. "Those people remind me of the bandits in the Wild West that I've always heard about—the ones who robbed stagecoaches."

"That sounds about right."

Dean tapped his screen, and the reporter's voice disappeared.

He'd downloaded the local newscast to listen to on the drive. He could see that was a mistake. Instead, he hit another button and "I'll Be Home for Christmas" filled his red F150 instead.

Much better.

In some ways, this stretch of desert felt like America's final frontier. It was still untamed with its own brand of justice.

Kota shifted beside him, crossing her jean-clad legs as she got comfortable. "I was reading a book the other day about the Old West, and the author talked about how rich people traveling from the East actually *wanted* to get robbed when they came out for a visit. It became somewhat of a rite of passage. They'd even get their pictures taken with the robbers so they could show the photos to their friends at home. Isn't that crazy?"

Dean smiled, enjoying hearing her talk. Their conversations had been pretty generic since they'd met eight months ago. Mostly, they talked about cooking and cleaning—since that's what he and Kota did for a living.

They saw each other almost every day, but so far he only knew a few things about her. She mostly kept to herself.

But he liked getting to know her better. He really liked hearing her talk about something other than work. Maybe she was finally coming out of her shell.

"Yes, the whole situation with the Roadside Bandits is crazy," he finally said. "I try to stay away from trouble. I definitely don't invite it into my life."

"Smart man." Kota rubbed her arms and stared out the window as the sun began to sink lower in the sky. Maybe they'd get a pretty sunset tonight. There was nothing like a desert sunset with its layers of rich colors.

The barren landscape stretched for miles and miles around them. The road ahead of them wound through the land like a piece of Christmas garland that had been abandoned.

The last car they'd passed had been twenty miles back.

This area was truly off grid.

Dean, originally an Alabama boy, loved it here in western Arizona. The landscape was ever changing. Sometimes flat. Sometimes hilly. Sometimes cut with dry canyons. Sometimes there was no foliage, and sometimes the landscape was dotted with sagebrush and agave or Joshua trees.

He often felt as if he'd been transported to another world out here.

Vanishing Ranch, where he worked as chef, was in the middle of nowhere—for good reason. But that meant he had to drive three hours to get to the specialty store to find the ingredients he needed for Christmas dinner. Then they had to drive another three hours on the return trip.

He and Kota still had an hour and a half until they'd be back at the ranch.

Sure, there were closer stores. But to get exactly what he needed, he'd had to go farther.

It was time consuming, but he was glad he had company on this trip.

He glanced at Kota as she studied a picture in her hands.

He grinned when he saw it.

Someone on the sidewalk outside the grocery store had been offering Polaroid photos in front of a cactus decorated with Christmas lights. Dean had insisted the two of them have a picture taken together. He'd made a nice donation to the vagabond who'd been trying to raise some money. He liked to help others whenever he could.

In the photo, Dean stood with one arm around Kota and the other offering a thumbs up, Kota grinned sweetly as she tilted her head at the photographer.

The woman had always reminded him of Selma Hayek with her pleasant features, slim frame, and long, dark hair.

She was beautiful and sweet with a killer smile.

But he could also see the pain behind her eyes, and he knew there was more to her story.

There was more to everyone's story, wasn't there? His included.

"So, are you happy now?" Kota lowered the picture, leaving it on the seat between them. "You have the ingredients for that turkey-fluffin you've been talking up for the past several weeks."

"Turducken," he corrected. "Turkey-duck-chicken."

Yes, he'd been talking it up at the ranch. He loved

discussing food because food bonded people, and eating meals together at a common table helped to build community. He saw his job as a ministry of sorts.

Kota cast a smile his way. "You're really going all out for your Christmas meal. Doesn't it take like five or six hours to prepare the tur-duffin?"

"Turducken." He chuckled. "Yeah, about that long, and another twelve hours to roast it."

"I can't imagine."

"I roast it at a hundred fifty degrees. Comes out juicy and tender. Only the best for the residents at Vanishing Ranch." That's what he always told himself.

The guests there had been through awful experiences, and Dean wanted to do everything he could to ensure they'd enjoy a nice Christmas at their new home away from home. Whatever he could do to help . . .

Christmas was tomorrow. Yes, tomorrow. He'd intended on buying everything he needed earlier in the month. But things had been busy with several new residents joining them—the holidays seemed to bring out the worst in some people—and Dean hadn't had a chance to get away.

He was grateful Kota had blessed him with her company on the trip. Really, she'd come out of convenience. There were a few things she'd wanted to pick up in town also, so she'd caught a ride.

Dean wasn't complaining.

No woman had turned his head—not since his sweet Angelica had died from cancer three years ago. But there was something fascinating about Kota. She never wanted any attention for herself, she never complained, and she always seemed grateful.

His mama used to say that a person couldn't be sad and grateful at the same time. As usual, his mama was right.

Just as they were about to round a bend in the desolate road, a pop sounded.

The next instant, his truck began to bounce.

His steering wheel fought against him, jerking to the side.

His jaw tightened. "You've got to be kidding me . . ."

Kota's eyes widened with alarm as she glanced at him. "What is it?"

He frowned before bringing his truck to a stop and throwing it in Park. "I think I just blew a tire."

"What?" Her voice caught as she looked around at the landscape.

The landscape devoid of civilization.

"Stay here." He opened his door and stepped out.

The fifty-degree late afternoon greeted him. Right

now, it was calm outside, but forecasters were calling for some unseasonable weather later. That was just another reason he wanted to get back to the ranch as soon as possible.

Dean walked toward the back of his truck, shaking his head as he anticipated what he'd find.

Sure enough, his tire was flat as a pancake.

How in the world had that happened? His tires had plenty of tread left on them. He routinely maintained the correct air pressure.

He always took care of his vehicles. Maybe it was his military background. His years of service had turned him from an unmotivated teen into a disciplined soldier. Those traits served him well now.

He shook his head, his hands on his hips as he made his way back to his door. The song on his phone had changed, and now "Rockin' Around the Christmas Tree" drifted out—such a cheery tune for the moment.

He leaned inside toward Kota. "Turns out we do have a slight problem—a flat tire. Thankfully, I have a spare in the back, but it's going to take a few moments to fix it."

She had her phone out and squinted as she stared at it. "Unfortunately, we don't have a signal out here."

Dean wasn't surprised. Many areas in the middle of the desert had no cell phone service.

"We'll be okay," he told her. "Let me just get this tire changed, and we'll be on our way."

He reached into the truck and cut the engine, shoving the keys into his pocket. He wanted to conserve all the gas he could.

But as he started toward the back of the truck, he paused.

In the far distance, he spotted another vehicle heading their way.

Maybe the newscast he'd just been listening to was messing with his mind because Dean wasn't usually one to jump to ominous thoughts.

But when he saw two men hanging out from the truck bed, a bad feeling began brewing in his gut.

He had a feeling these guys wouldn't be stopping to help them.

No, they'd stop to start trouble.

**Click Here to Read More!**

# COMPLETE BOOK LIST

**Squeaky Clean Mysteries:**

    #1 Hazardous Duty

    #2 Suspicious Minds

    #2.5 It Came Upon a Midnight Crime (novella)

    #3 Organized Grime

    #4 Dirty Deeds

    #5 The Scum of All Fears

    #6 To Love, Honor and Perish

    #7 Mucky Streak

    #8 Foul Play

    #9 Broom & Gloom

    #10 Dust and Obey

    #11 Thrill Squeaker

    #11.5 Swept Away (novella)

    #12 Cunning Attractions

    #13 Cold Case: Clean Getaway

#14 Cold Case: Clean Sweep

#15 Cold Case: Clean Break

#16 Cleans to an End

While You Were Sweeping, A Riley Thomas Spinoff


**The Sierra Files:**

#1 Pounced

#2 Hunted

#3 Pranced

#4 Rattled


**The Gabby St. Claire Diaries (a Tween Mystery series):**

The Curtain Call Caper

The Disappearing Dog Dilemma

The Bungled Bike Burglaries


**The Worst Detective Ever**

#1 Ready to Fumble

#2 Reign of Error

#3 Safety in Blunders

#4 Join the Flub

#5 Blooper Freak

#6 Flaw Abiding Citizen

#7 Gaffe Out Loud

#8 Joke and Dagger

#9 Wreck the Halls

#10 Glitch and Famous

**Raven Remington**

Relentless

**Holly Anna Paladin Mysteries:**

#1 Random Acts of Murder

#2 Random Acts of Deceit

#2.5 Random Acts of Scrooge

#3 Random Acts of Malice

#4 Random Acts of Greed

#5 Random Acts of Fraud

#6 Random Acts of Outrage

#7 Random Acts of Iniquity

**Lantern Beach Mysteries**

#1 Hidden Currents

#2 Flood Watch

#3 Storm Surge

#4 Dangerous Waters

#5 Perilous Riptide

#6 Deadly Undertow

**Lantern Beach Romantic Suspense**

Tides of Deception

Shadow of Intrigue

Storm of Doubt
Winds of Danger
Rains of Remorse
Torrents of Fear

**Lantern Beach P.D.**
On the Lookout
Attempt to Locate
First Degree Murder
Dead on Arrival
Plan of Action

**Lantern Beach Escape**
Afterglow (a novelette)

**Lantern Beach Blackout**
Dark Water
Safe Harbor
Ripple Effect
Rising Tide

**Lantern Beach Guardians**
Hide and Seek
Shock and Awe
Safe and Sound

**Lantern Beach Blackout: The New Recruits**

Rocco

Axel

Beckett

Gabe

**Lantern Beach Mayday**

Run Aground

Dead Reckoning

Tipping Point

**Lantern Beach Blackout: Danger Rising**

Brandon

Dylan

Maddox

Titus

**Lantern Beach Christmas**

Silent Night

**Crime á la Mode**

Dead Man's Float

Milkshake Up

Bomb Pop Threat

Banana Split Personalities

**Beach Bound Books and Beans Mysteries**

Bound by Murder

Bound by Disaster
Bound by Mystery
Bound by Trouble

## Vanishing Ranch

Forgotten Secrets
Necessary Risk
Risky Ambition
Deadly Intent
Lethal Betrayal
High Stakes Deception
Fatal Vendetta
Troubled Tidings (coming soon)

## The Sidekick's Survival Guide

The Art of Eavesdropping
The Perks of Meddling
The Exercise of Interfering
The Practice of Prying
The Skill of Snooping
The Craft of Being Covert

## Saltwater Cowboys

Saltwater Cowboy
Breakwater Protector
Cape Corral Keeper
Seagrass Secrets

Driftwood Danger

Unwavering Security

## Beach House Mysteries

The Cottage on Ghost Lane

The Inn on Hanging Hill

The House on Dagger Point

## School of Hard Rocks Mysteries

The Treble with Murder

Crime Strikes a Chord

Tone Death

## Carolina Moon Series

Home Before Dark

Gone By Dark

Wait Until Dark

Light the Dark

Taken By Dark

## Suburban Sleuth Mysteries:

Death of the Couch Potato's Wife

## Fog Lake Suspense:

Edge of Peril

Margin of Error

Brink of Danger

Line of Duty
Legacy of Lies
Secrets of Shame
Refuge of Redemption

**Cape Thomas Series:**
Dubiosity
Disillusioned
Distorted

**Standalone Romantic Mystery:**
The Good Girl

**Suspense:**
Imperfect
The Wrecking

**Sweet Christmas Novella:**
Home to Chestnut Grove

**Standalone Romantic-Suspense:**
Keeping Guard
The Last Target
Race Against Time
Ricochet
Key Witness
Lifeline

High-Stakes Holiday Reunion

Desperate Measures

Hidden Agenda

Mountain Hideaway

Dark Harbor

Shadow of Suspicion

The Baby Assignment

The Cradle Conspiracy

Trained to Defend

Mountain Survival

Dangerous Mountain Rescue

**Nonfiction:**

Characters in the Kitchen

Changed: True Stories of Finding God through Christian Music (out of print)

The Novel in Me: The Beginner's Guide to Writing and Publishing a Novel (out of print)

# ABOUT THE AUTHOR

*USA Today* has called Christy Barritt's books "scary, funny, passionate, and quirky."

Christy writes both mystery and romantic suspense novels that are clean with underlying messages of faith. Her books have sold more than three million copies and have won the Daphne du Maurier Award for Excellence in Suspense and Mystery, have been twice nominated for the Romantic Times Reviewers' Choice Award, and have finaled for both a Carol Award and Foreword Magazine's Book of the Year.

She is married to her Prince Charming, a man who thinks she's hilarious—but only when she's not trying to be. Christy is a self-proclaimed klutz, an avid music lover who's known for spontaneously bursting into song, and a road trip aficionado.

When she's not working or spending time with her family, she enjoys singing, playing the guitar, and exploring small, unsuspecting towns where people have no idea how accident-prone she is.

Find Christy online at:
    **www.christybarritt.com**
    **www.facebook.com/christybarritt**
    **www.twitter.com/cbarritt**

Sign up for Christy's newsletter to get information on all of her latest releases here: **www.christybarritt. com/newsletter-sign-up/**

www.ingramcontent.com/pod-product-compliance
Lightning Source LLC
Chambersburg PA
CBHW031957150726
47990CB00005B/1750